John Edward Gray, George Robert Gray

Catalogue of the Mammalia and Birds of New Guinea, in the Collection of the British Museum

SALZWASSER VERLAG

John Edward Gray, George Robert Gray

Catalogue of the Mammalia and Birds of New Guinea, in the Collection of the British Museum

Reprint of the original, first published in 1859.

1st Edition 2022 | ISBN: 978-3-37513-216-3

Verlag (Publisher): Salzwasser Verlag GmbH, Zeilweg 44, 60439 Frankfurt, Deutschland
Vertretungsberechtigt (Authorized to represent): E. Roepke, Zeilweg 44, 60439 Frankfurt, Deutschland
Druck (Print): Books on Demand GmbH, In de Tarpen 42, 22848 Norderstedt, Deutschland

CATALOGUE

OF THE

MAMMALIA AND BIRDS

OF

NEW GUINEA,

IN THE COLLECTION OF THE

BRITISH MUSEUM.

BY

JOHN EDWARD GRAY, Ph.D., F.R.S.,

AND

GEORGE ROBERT GRAY, F.L.S., etc

LONDON:

PRINTED BY ORDER OF THE TRUSTEES.

1859.

PREFACE.

THIS Catalogue gives a list of all the specimens of Mammalia and Birds received from New Guinea, now in the Collection of the British Museum, and a list of the species which have been received from that country contained in other Collections, but which are now desiderata to the Museum.

Tables are added showing the geographical distribution of the species of New Guinea and other neighbouring islands, and of the species found in those islands which have not yet been observed in New Guinea,—the specimens which are in the Museum from these various localities being marked by a double star (**).

Descriptions are given of several species which appear not to have been hitherto recorded.

JOHN EDWARD GRAY.

1 Dec. 1858.

CATALOGUE

OF THE

MAMMALS AND BIRDS

OF

NEW GUINEA.

MAMMALIA.

Fam. VESPERTILIONIDÆ.

HIPPOSIDEROS.

As M. Bonaparte has given the name of *Phyllorhina* to the European Horse-shoe Bats, the genus *Hipposideros* may be confined to those species of the larger genus which have a large cavity opening with an expanding pore on the forehead behind the transverse hinder part of the nose-leaf (they have distinct pubal teats), thus restricting *Phyllorhina* to those which have a simple forehead without any pore.

HIPPOSIDEROS ARUENSIS.

Hipposideros Aruensis, J. E. Gray, Proc. Zool. Soc. 1858.

Sooty-brown; the lower half of the hairs of the back paler; the hairs of the under side more uniform, or with rather paler tips; the ears large, broad, rounded at the ends, with two hairy lines on the inner side of the front edge; face and chin rather bristly, without any membranaceous ridges on the sides outside of the nose-leaf.

Hab. Aru Islands (*Wallace*).

a. Male. Aru Island.

Length of head and body 2''; tail $\frac{5}{8}$; expanse of wings $5\frac{1}{4}$; length of upper arm bone $1\frac{1}{2}$; length of shin bone $\frac{5}{8}$ inch.

The ears sooty-black; the front margin of the ears is broad, with a rounded lobe on the basal part near the forehead; wings broad, thin, sooty-black, bald ; thumb slender, of two subequal joints ; the interfemoral membrane broad, truncate at the end ; the hind legs slender, rather elongate ; feet slender, enveloped in the membrane to the base of the slender equal compressed toes ; the heel-bones elongate, longer than the foot ; tail elongate, slender, attached, and extending a little beyond the end of the truncated interfemoral membrane.

Cutting teeth $\frac{1-1}{4}$; upper large, chisel-shaped, separated by a small space from each other and from the canines ; the lower small, crowded, three-lobed ; canines conical ; grinders —— ?

The specimen is unfortunately rather injured about the face ; but it appears quite distinct in form from any of the Horse-shoe Bats I have hitherto observed.

This species appears to be quite distinct from *Hipposideros speoris* of Timor, which is described as being a little larger than the larger English Horse-shoe Bat, *Phyllorhina bifer* ; it has the following synonyma :—

Vespertilio speoris, Schneid. in Schreb. Säugth. t. 59 B. ; Shaw, Zool. i. 147.

Rhinolophus marsupialis, Geoff. Cour. 1805.

Rhinolophus speoris, Geoff. Ann. Mus. xx. 261. t. 5. 266 ; Desm. N. D. H. N. xl. 368 ; Mam. 126 ; Fischer, Mam. 139.

Rhinolophe cruménifère, Péron & Lesueur, Voy. aux Terres Aust. Atlas, i. t. 35.

Hab. Timor (*Péron* and *Lesueur*).

It is certainly distinct from *Hipposideros insignis*, Gray, Mag. Zool. & Bot. ii. 492, the *Rhinolophus insignis*, Horsf. Java, *Vesp. cyclope*, Deschamps, MSS., from Java, which Fischer confounded with the former, and which has acute ears on the sides of the face, numerous lamellæ under the front part of the nose-leaf, and is 13¼ inches in expanse of wings.

PTEROPUS ARGENTATUS.

Pteropus argentatus, Gray, Proc. Zool. Soc. 1858.

Back white, with scattered black hairs ; beneath yellowish ; face grey, nakedish ; head deeper yellow-grey, with black interspersed hairs ; collar broad, bright red-chestnut, darker brown at the sides and under side, where the hair is longer, forming a kind of ruff ; ears and membranes (when dry) black.

Hab. Aru Island (*Wallace*).

a. Female. Aru Island.

"Back of a silky or silvery shining white, very beautiful in the freshly killed animals."—*Wallace*.

Order FERÆ.

Tribe Viverrina.

Fam. FELIDÆ.

PARADOXURUS HERMAPHRODITA.

Viverra nigra, Desm. Mam.
Viverra hermaphrodita, Pallas.
Paradoxurus typus, F. Cuv. Mam. Lithog.; Temm. Monog. ii.
315; Gray, List Mam. B.M. 56.
Platychista Pallasii, Otto, Nov. Act. Leop. xvii. t. 71, 72.
Paradoxurus hermaphrodita, Gray, Proc. Zool. Soc. 1858.
Hab. Ké Islands (*Wallace*).
a. Ké Islands.

Fam. MACROPODIDÆ.

a. *Phalangistina.*

BELIDEUS ARIEL.

Belidea Ariel, Gould, Proc. Zool. Soc. 1842, x. 11; Ann. & Mag.
N. H. 1842, 404; Gray, Proc. Zool. Soc. 1858.
Petaurus sciureus, Müller, Verhand. tabl.
Petaurus Ariel, Gray, List Mam. B.M. 84.
Hab. Aru Island (*Wallace*); Port Essington (*Gould*).
a. Female adult, with one young in the pouch. Aru Island.

CUSCUS.

Herr Temminck, in the first volume of the 'Monographies de
Mammalogie,' published in 1827, divides the short hairy-eared kinds,
Cusci, into three species.

At the time he wrote he only had specimens from the northern
part of Celebes, brought home by Professor Reinhardt, and from
the islands of Banda and Amboyna.

These species evidently depend principally on the colour of the
fur, which appears to be very variable in different individuals. It is
true that he describes and figures skulls of the different individuals;
but the difference between those of *Phalangista chrysorrhos* and *P.
maculata* appears chiefly to depend on the age and development of
the specimen figured. M. Temminck and the writers of his school
always forget that the skull and other parts of the skeleton are
liable to quite as much variation from local circumstances, food,
and other accidental causes, as the colour of the fur or the size of
the animal. M. Temminck characterizes them thus:—

1. In *Phalangista ursina* the fur is thicker and closer, and the
long hairs thicker than in the other species, blackish, with yellow
tips to the longer hairs; and the forehead of the skull is flat. Of this
he had several specimens of different ages, all brought by Professor

Reinhardt from the northern part of Celebes, the natives of which have not observed any varieties in colouring.

2. *P. chrysorrhos* is described from two specimens brought home by the same Professor, from some of the Moluccas, which have a short cottony fur, of an ash-grey more or less black, and the rump and upper part of the base of the tail golden-yellow.

3. Of *P. maculata* Herr Temminck particularly observes, that the fur in all ages and in both sexes is covered with irregular white or brown spots, which are paler and less marked in the young. The very young are sometimes entirely ashy. They come from Banda and Amboyna.

The yellow colour of the rump and the base of the tail, as far as the specimens in the British Museum show, is common to the ashy specimens, which might be called *P. chrysorrhos*, and the variegated specimens, which might be named *P. maculata*: it is very difficult to distinguish the pale-rumped ashy ones from those without that mark; but it is easy to connect the grey or ashy-spotted ones with either the one or the other; and it is impossible to separate the ashy-grey spotted ones from the brown or orange spotted specimens. In one specimen the animal is nearly white, with some small dark spots about an inch over; and in another the animal is white, with red feet, and one large red spot on the middle of the back.

From the examination of the specimens in the British Museum, and of their skulls, I am inclined to believe that the *P. ursina* is distinct, and that *P. chrysorrhos* and *P. maculata* are varieties of the same species.

Mr. Wallace having sent two specimens of this genus to the British Museum, to determine them I went over the previous observations on the genus, and examined the numerous specimens which are in the Museum collection, received from the French voyages of discovery, Mr. J. Macgillivray, the Naturalist of H.M. Ship 'Rattlesnake,' and those now sent from the Island of Ula; and I have come to the belief that they are all to be referred to four species, which are very variable in the colour of the fur; one being variable in both the sexes, and the other, in which the sexes differ greatly from each other, but appear to be permanent in their colour; one species in which the furs of the two sexes are alike and uniform in colour; and one, of which the female sex only is known, which is uniform iron-grey.

The two have the ears small, hairy on both sides, and hidden in the fur; the other two have larger ears, exposed beyond the fur and bald within.

1. Cuscus maculatus.

Phalanger, male, Buffon, H. N. xiii. t. 11.

Phalangista maculata, Desm. N. D. H. N. xxv. 472; Temm. Monog. i. 14. t. 3. f. 1–6; Quoy & Gaim. Voy. Uran. Zool. 59. t. 7; Waterh. Mamm. i. 274. f.

Phalangista ursina, part., Waterh. Mamm. 267.

Phalangista chrysorrhos, Temm. Monog. i. 12; Waterh. Mamm. i. 271.

Cuscus maculatus, Lesson & Garnot, Voy. Coq. Zool. 150. t. 4 ; Gray, Proc. Zool. Soc. 1858.

Cuscus macrourus, Lesson & Garnot, Voy. Coq. Zool. i. 156. t. 5 ; Waterh. Mamm. i. 277.

Ears almost hidden in the fur, clothed internally and externally with fur ; forehead convex ; forehead of the skull convex and rounded in front ; grinders moderate ; fur ashy-grey, or white and grey, or reddish, varied or spotted. Rump and base of the tail yellowish-white.

Hab. New Guinea (*Macgillivray*) ; Aru Island (*Wallace*) ; Molucca, Island of Waygeroo (*Verreaux*).

a. Adult female, from the Moluccas, from the Leyden Museum, sent as *C. chrysorrhos.* Uniform ashy-grey ; face, throat, chest, and beneath the rump and base of the tail yellowish.

b. Young female, from the south coast of New Guinea. Presented by J. B. Jukes, Esq. Dark blackish-ashy ; head, neck and shoulders paler ; rump and base of the tail reddish-yellow ; cheeks, throat and beneath white ; feet bright red.

The two sides of this specimen are not coloured alike. The forehead of the *skull* is very convex.

c. Half-grown "male from Darnley Island, brought from the south coast of New Guinea." Presented by J. Macgillivray, Esq. Reddish ; back and thighs darker blackish-ashy ; cheeks, throat, under side, large confluent spots on the sides, the rump and tail white ; feet bright red. Like *Cuscus maculatus,* Quoy and Gaimard, Voy. Uranie, t. 7.

d. Half-grown "male from New Guinea." Presented by J. Macgillivray, Esq. Like the former, but white, with irregular large symmetrical pale reddish spots on body, limbs and tail.

e. Half-grown "female from Dufaure Island, south coast of New Guinea." Presented by John Macgillivray, Esq. Like the former, but white, with one very large reddish spot on the hinder part of the back ; two large spots on the hind legs, and an obscured indication of a large patch on the shoulders ; the feet red.

f. Half-grown, from the "island of Waygeroo." From M. Verreaux. Ashy-grey cheeks ; back with some white spots ; throat, chest, belly, rump and tail white ; sides white, with scattered, round, nearly equal-sized spots ; feet reddish.

g. Adult male. Aru Island. Sent by Mr. Wallace. White ; body and limbs with small, roundish, rarely confluent, ashy-black spots ; feet white : the skull has a very convex forehead.

Cuscus maculatus, Lesson, Voy. Coq. t. 4, is intermediate in colour and marking between Nos. *g* and *c.*

Cuscus macrourus, Lesson, Voy. Coq. t. 5, from the island of Waygeroo, bears a great similarity to No. *c* ; but the reddish spots are less confluent.

The figure of *C. Quoyi,* in Quoy and Gaimard, Voy. Uranie, t. 6,

looks like a specimen of this species intermediate between the ashy
and spotted variety, being ashy with darker obscure spots.

Chrysorrhos would perhaps be the better name for this species,
because all I have seen have a yellow rump and base of the tail; but
some are not spotted.

2. CUSCUS ORIENTALIS.

♀ ♂ *Phalangista cavifrons*, Temm. Monog. i. 17.

♀ ♂ *Cuscus orientalis*, Gray, List Mamm. B.M. 84; Proc. Zool.
Soc. 1858, t. 61.

♀ ♂ *Phalangista (Cuscus) orientalis*, Waterh. Mamm. i. 279.

♂ *Coescoes*, Valentyn, Omst. in Amboyna, iii. 272.

Phalanger, Penn. Quadr. ii. 27.

♂ *Didelphis orientalis*, Pallas, Misc. Zool. 59; Schreb. Säugth.
iii. 550. t. 152.

♂ *Cuscus Amboinensis*, Lacép.

♂ *Phalangista alba*, Geoff. Cat. Mus.

♂ *Cuscus albus*, Lesson & Garnot, Voy. Coq. Zool. i. 158. t. 6.

♂ *Balantia orientalis*, Illíger, Prodr. 78.

♀ *Phalangista rufa*, Geoff. Cat. Mus.; Desm. N. D. H. N. xxv.
473.

♀ *Phalanger*, female, Buffon, H. N. xiii. t. 10.

Cuscus Quoyii, Lesson, Mamm. 226.

Phalangista Quoyi, Quoy & Gaim. Voy. Uranie, Zool. 58. t. 6 ? ?;
Temm. Mon. Mamm. i. 17.

Phalangista Papuensis, Desm. Mamm. Supp. ii. 541; Bull. Sci.
Nat. iii. 64.

Phalangista (Cuscus) maculata, part., Waterhouse, Mamm. i. 275.

? *Cuscus albus*, Lesson, Voy. Coq. t. 6, ♂ ?

Ears produced beyond the fur, naked internally; forehead concave. Male white. Female pale reddish-brown, with a darker
longitudinal streak; skull with a narrow concave forehead; grinders
moderate.

Hab. New Guinea; Aru Island (*Wallace*).

a. Adult male, from New Ireland, procured from M. Verreaux of
Paris; said to have come from one of the expeditions. Pure white;
throat yellow; feet nearly bald.

b. A nearly adult male, from the old collection, said to have come
from Amboyna. White.

c. Young male? Uniform pale brownish-yellow; throat, chest
and belly whiter. From island of Waygeroo; procured from M. Verreaux of Paris.

d. Adult female: ashy-brown, glistened with silvery; throat,
chest and belly pure white; back with a narrow uniform longitudinal
streak. This is sent as *Cuscus Quoyii*, Lesson, Mam. 220; *Ph.
Papuensis* of Desmarest, Supp. The figure of M. Gaimard's animal
in the ' Voyage of the Uranie,' t. 6, is more like a variety of *C. ursinus*; but the description agrees with our animal.

e. Young female, from the island of Waygeroo; procured from
M. Verreaux.

f. Young female, from Aru Islands; procured from Mr. A. R. Wallace. These two only differ from the adult specimen in the silvery hairs of the 'back being rather more abundant, but they seem to be deciduous.

Phalangista Papuensis of Desm. was described from a female specimen collected by M. Gaimard, which was afterwards described as *Ph. Quoyi.* In Quoy and Gaimard, 'Zoology to the Voyage of the Uranie,' it is described as having a darker dorsal line, which rather widens over the loins, which at once shows that it must be the female of *P. orientalis.*

Mr. Waterhouse has referred both these names without any comment as a synonym of *P. maculata,* misled probably by Herr Temminck, who (Mon. Mamm. i. 18) states it to be a young *P. maculata*—evidently overlooking the dorsal stripe.

Lesson, in the 'Voyage of the Coquille,' figures a male animal as *Cuscus albus,* t. 6, from Port Praslin, New Ireland, which is white, with a narrow black streak, just as in the female of this species.

Knowing the little reliance that is often to be placed on M. Lesson's figures, I suspect it is the figure of a pale or perhaps bleached specimen of a female *P. orientalis,* in which some fold of the pouch, probably produced from bad stuffing, has been mistaken by'the artist for the scrotum of a male.

3. CUSCUS BREVICAUDATUS.

Phalangista nudicaudata, Gould, Proc. Zool. Soc. 1849, p. 110.
Cuscus brevicaudatus, Gray, Proc. Zool. Soc. 1858.

The ears hid in the fur, woolly internally and externally; tail short; the forehead ——? ; the front lower cutting-teeth broad.

Female uniform ashy-grey; rump and base of tail, throat, chest and belly yellowish dirty-white.

Hab. Australia, Cape York.

a. "A female two-thirds grown, from Cape York." Presented by John Macgillivray, Esq,

The only specimen known is very like the ashy variety of *C. maculatus,* but the front lower cutting-teeth are much broader, and the tail, which has the bones still remaining on it, is considerably shorter than any of our specimens of *C. maculatus.*

The specimen in the British Museum is that described by Mr. Gould.

Mr. Gould refers this animal to the subgenus *Pseudocheirus* of the genus *Phalangista,* and calls it *P. nudicaudata,* because it " differs from all the other Australian members of the genus in having the apical three-fourths of its tail entirely destitute of hair." But Mr. Gould overlooked the fact that it is not a *Pseudocheirus,* but a *Cuscus,* all the species of which have the major part of the tail naked; and the species under consideration has the naked part of the tail, and indeed the tail itself, shorter than the rest of the species; so that the specific name of *nudicaudata* is singularly inapplicable.

The light mark on the rump, which Mr. Gould compared to that of the *Koala*, is also common to the species of *Cuscus*, and is probably produced by the habit of the animal sitting on its rump, rolled up into a ball, on the fork of the branches of treés.

The skull shows that the animal is much younger than the label indicates, as it appears only to have the milk teeth, and the broad lower incisors of the younger specimens of this genus. The skull differs both from that of *C. ursinus* and *C. maculatus*, but it is too young to predict what may be the normal form of the adult animal.

The front half of the space between the eyes is rather convex, but not nearly so much so as the young skull of *C. maculatus*; and the front of the forehead just behind the convexity described is rather concave; this concavity has no resemblance to the deep concavity occupying nearly the whole space between the eyes in *C. ursinus* and *C. maculatus*.

4. CUSCUS URSINUS.

Phalangista (Ceonix) ursina, Temm. Monog. i. 10. t. 1. f. 1–3; t. 2. f. 1–5, skull; t. 3, skeleton; Lesson, Cent. Zool. t. 10; Waterhouse, Mamm. i. 267, part.

Cuscus ursinus, Gray, Proc. Zool. Soc. 1858.

Ears almost hidden in the fur, clothed with fur internally and externally; fur blackish-ash, with larger silvery hairs; head, throat, belly and tail rather pale brown; forehead flat, concave; forehead of the skull flat, deeply concave; grinders large, in a strongly-arched series.

Hab. Celebes.

a. The specimen with its skull, which was obtained from the Zoological Society, and is the specimen described by Mr. Waterhouse in Mammalia, i. p. 268.

The other specimen there indicated as being in the British Museum is a young example of *C. maculatus*.

In Lesson's figure in Cent. Zool. t. 10, it is represented as uniform blackish-brown, with rather large white-edged ears!

The larger size of the teeth and the flatness of the forehead of the skull at once separate this from *C. maculatus*.

5. CUSCUS CELEBENSIS.

Ears produced beyond the fur, naked internally. Male and female alike, ashy-grey, grizzled with silvery hairs; the nape and the upper part of the middle of the back blacker, but without any distinct dorsal streak.

Cuscus Celebensis, Brit. Mus.; Gray, Proc. Zool. Soc. 1858, t. 62.

Hab. Celebes; Macassar (*Wallace*); San Cristoval (*Macgillivray*).

a. Young animal, from the island of Macassar. Procured from Mr. J. R. Wallace in 1851.

b. Adult male and female, from San Cristoval, Soloman Group of Islands, Dec. 1855. Presented by John Macgillivray, Esq. and F. M. Rayner, Esq. in 1856.

b. *Macropina.*

DENDROLAGUS URSINUS.

Dendrolagus ursinus, S. Müller, Verh. 131, 141. t. 19. f. 22, 23 ;
Gould, Macrop. t. 25 ; Gray, List Mam. B.M. 87.
Hypsiprymnus ursinus, Temm. Faun. Japon. 6.
Hab. New Guinea (*Müller*).
a. New Guinea. From the Leyden Museum.

DENDROLAGUS INUSTUS.

Dendrolagus inustus, S. Müller, Verh. 131, 143. t. 20, 22, 23 ;
Gould, Macrop. t. .
Hypsiprymnus inustus, Temm. Faun. Japon. 6.
Hab. New Guinea (*Müller*).
a. New Guinea. From the Leyden Museum.

DORCOPSIS ASIATICUS.

Filander or Kangaroo, Le Brun's Voyage, i. 347. t. 213, 1714.
Didelphis Asiaticus, Pallas, N. A. Petrop. 1777, 228. t. 9 ; Voy.
Astrol. t. .
Didelphis Brunii, Gmelin, S. N. i. 109 ; Cuv. Tabl. Elem. 1798.
Halmaturus Asiaticus, Gray, List Mam. B.M. 91.
Halmaturus Brunii, Illiger, Prod.
Hypsiprymnus Brunii, Müller, Verh. 63. t. 21–23.
Dorcopsis Brunii, Müller, Verhand. 131.
Dorcopsis Asiaticus, Gray, Voy. Sam. 32.
Hab. Island of Aru.

It is curious that this animal, described as specially inhabiting the island visited by Mr. Wallace, was not sent home by him. It is to be hoped that he did not neglect it, thinking it a common Kangaroo, as it is a desideratum in most museums in Europe.
a. " Aru Island." From the Leyden Museum.

c. *Peramelina.*

PERAMELES (ECHIMIPERA) DOREYANUS.

Perameles Doreyanus, Quoy & Gaimard, Voy. Astrol. Zool. i. 100.
t. 16. f. 1–5 ; Waterhouse, Mamm. i. 386.
Echymipera Kalulu, Lesson, Règne Anim. 192.

Tail naked, rugose, squamose, wrinkled below. Toes 3·5 : the two inner front large, equal ; the outer small ; the inner hind toe short, clawless ; the two index fingers small, united, clawed.
Hab. Aru Island (*Wallace*).
a. Female. Aru Island.

"The skin is very thin and friable.
"Teeth 46 :—Inc. $\frac{8}{6}$; C. $\frac{1-1}{1-1}$; Prem. $\frac{3-3}{3-3}$; M. $\frac{4-4}{4-4}$."—*Wallace.*

This enumeration agrees with that given by MM. Quoy and Gaimard, being two cutting teeth in the upper jaw less than are found in the other species of the genus ; hence Lesson considered it as forming a distinct genus. The outer and inner toes of the fore-feet are very small, rudimentary and clawless.

d. *Dasyurina.*

PHASCOGALE (ANTECHINUS) MELAS.

Phascogale (*Antechinus*) *melas*, Müller, Verhand. t. 25. f. 1–3.
Hab. New Guinea (*Müller*).

The animal differs, according to the figure, in having the hair of the tail rather more elongated and spreading than the Australian species of the genus ; the dentition is more nearly allied to the *Antechinus* than to the new genus *Myoictis* sent home by Mr. Wallace.

MYOICTIS.

Myoictis, J. E. Gray, Proc. Zool. Soc. 1858.

Head tapering ; nose acute ; whiskers strong. Tail depressed, tapering, clothed with rather elongated hairs above and on the sides ; the under side flat, nakedish. Feet moderate ; soles bald to the heel ; toes 5·5, free, compressed ; claws acute ; first and fifth front toes equal ; second, third and fourth toes equal, longer ; hinder toes free, weak, distinct, clawless ; thumb of hind-foot larger. Ears roundish, nakedish. Scrotum pendulous.

Cutting teeth $\frac{4-4}{6}$; the upper with a central space in front between them, in a close series on each side, and with a small interspace between them and the canines ; the first tooth very small, hidden in the gums, the others all equal, lancet-shaped, rather crowded ; the lower forming a continued series, shelving forward, all lancet-shaped, subequal ; the front rather the longest and narrowest ; the hinder rather broader.

Canines $\frac{1-1}{1-1}$, conical ; the upper not quite developed, only slightly produced above the level of the other teeth ; the lower small, conical scarcely raised above the other teeth (figs. 3, 4).

False grinders $\frac{2-2}{2-2}$, conical, compressed ; the lower with a very obscure, the upper with a rather more distinct, conical tubercle on the front and hinder edge (figs. 3, 4).

True grinders $\frac{2-2}{3-3}$; the upper large, triangular, acutely lobed ; the lower compressed, very acutely lobed ; the middle one in each jaw the largest.

The angle of the lower jaw is produced, elongate and strongly inflexed, as is usual in *Marsupialia.*

Skull : length, 1 inch 3 lines ; width, all the zygomatic arch, 9 lines ; length of the tooth-line 9 lines. Length of the lower jaw $11\frac{1}{2}$, of symphysis $4\frac{1}{2}$, of tooth-line $7\frac{1}{2}$ lines (figs. 1, 2, 3, 4).

This genus is peculiar, because, as far as the dentition is concerned, there is no character by which we should have determined that it was a Marsupial animal ; but the form of the angle of the lower jaw at once shows its true affinity to that group. It was not until a most careful examination of the space between the front upper cutting teeth, that I could find any indication of the front pair of cutting teeth found in the allied genus *Antechinus*.

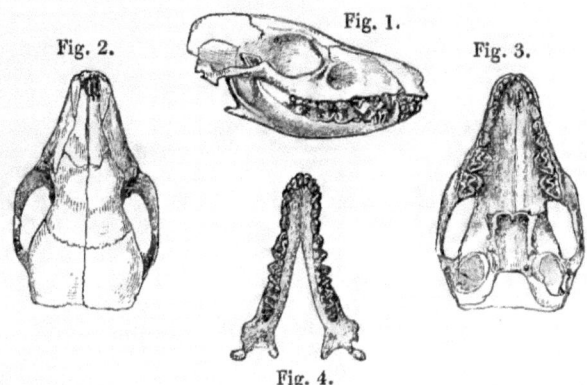

Fig. 1.

Fig. 2.

Fig. 3.

Fig. 4.

This genus is evidently allied to the genus *Antechinus* of Australia; but it is known at once by its external form, which is just that of a small Indian *Herpestes* or *Ichneumon*, having like that genus a depressed tail with long spreading hair, broad and depressed at the base, tapering to an acute tip which bears a pencil of hairs.

MYOICTIS WALLACII.

Myoictis Wallacii, Gray, Proc. Zool. Soc. 1858, t. 64.

Rusty-brown, with interspersed black longer hairs; head redder; throat, chest and belly pale reddish; side of the neck at the base of the ears bright reddish; ears, and the greater part of the tail bright red-brown; tip of the tail black.

Hab. Aru Island (*Wallace*).

Male. Aru Island.

"In houses as destructive as rats to everything eatable.

"Teeth 34:—Inc. $\frac{6}{6}$; C. $\frac{1-1}{1-1}$; Prem. $\frac{2-2}{2-2}$; M. $\frac{2-2}{3-3}$."—*Wallace*.

DACTYLOPSILA.

Dactylopsila, J. E. Gray, Proc. Zool. Soc. 1858.

Tail elongate, slender, depressed, densely clothed with fur, with the exception of the under side near the tip, which is bald and callous, the end rather bushy. Ears elongate, rounded, bald, except at the outer sides of the base. Pupil round? The fore-feet elongate; toes very slender, compressed, very unequal in length, quite free; the outer and third or middle toe nearly equal, the second or ring-finger much the longest, the fourth and fifth short, the fifth or innermost the shortest. The hind-feet slender, toes compressed, the two outer toes elongate, nearly equal, the two inner about half the length and united.

Skull (figs. 5, 6, 7) depressed, very broad, with very large expanded zygomatic arches; the face narrow, compressed and nearly erect on the sides, tapering in front; the palate narrow, concave. The cutting teeth $\frac{4-4}{4-4}$; the upper front elongate, projecting in front, rather tapering and truncated at the tip; the second and third compressed, chisel-shaped, close together and to the front; the second small, the third larger; the fourth separated from the others by a small space and placed on the intermaxillary suture, compressed, curved rather like a canine; the lower front very long, projecting in front, curved, rather tapering at the tip; the second, third and fourth small, truncated, separated from each other; the second largest, close to the base of the front tooth; the third small, separated from the second by a small space; the fourth very small, far from the other; and at the base of the front edge of the first grinder, in the space between the third and fourth on the right side of the jaw, is a cavity which appears to have been filled with a tooth like the third one, but there is no appearance of the tooth or cavity on the other side. Canines? $\frac{1-1}{0-0}$, upper small, compressed, conical, tapering like, but smaller than, what I have called the hinder cutting teeth (fig. 7). Grinders $\frac{5-5}{4-4}$, small, in two nearly straight lines parallel to each other, and the hinder ones in each jaw rather smaller than the front ones; the front upper small, triangular; the others four-sided and square, with four tubercles, the outer front tubercle of the second tooth being rather larger than the rest, which are nearly equal among themselves, and the front lower grinder has only one larger tubercle in the place of the two in the others (figs. 8, 9).

Fig. 5.   Fig. 6.

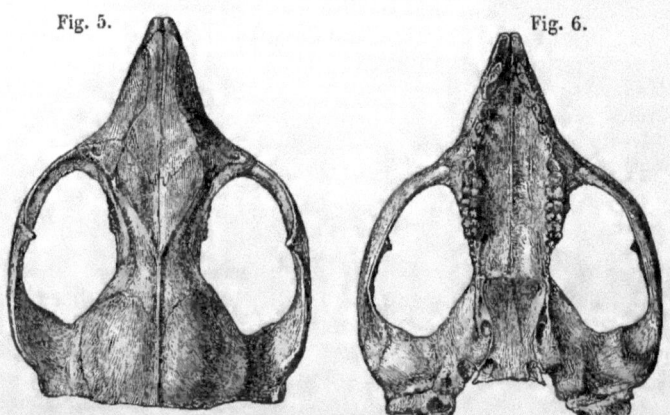

This genus is very distinct from the other genera of *Phalangistina*, in the elongated and depressed form of the tail, the formation of the fore-feet, and especially in the disposition and form of the teeth, as well as in the broad depressed skull.

The following observations may assist in showing the value of these characters.

Fig. 7.   Fig. 8.

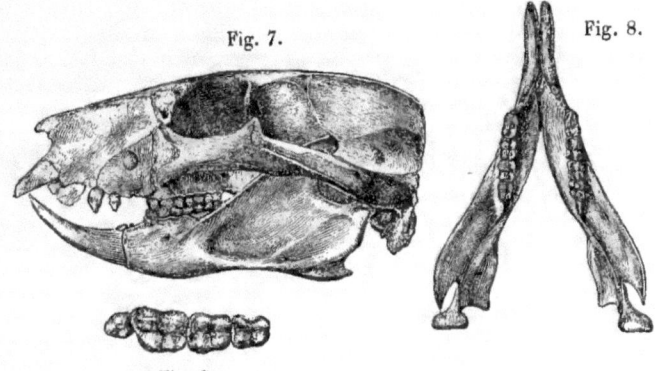

Fig. 9.

In *Cuscus* the fingers are rather longer than in *Hepoona*, and the third or middle finger is the longest, the others becoming gradually shorter on each side.

In *Phalangista* proper (that is *Trichosurus* of Mr. Waterhouse) the fingers are moderately long, the second and third are the longest and equal, the fourth longer than the first, and the fifth or inner one the shortest.

The hand of the *Hepoona* is very like that of *Phalangista*, both in the proportion and form of the fingers ; but the two inner fingers are rather separated and opposable to the other three.

The tail, though covered with hair, is very unlike those of the genera *Hepoona* and *Phalangista*, and is more like that of a squirrel, but not so bushy ; in *Hepoona* it is tapering and covered with shortish hair, and has a slender tip ; in the more perfect specimen of *Phalangista* it is cylindrical and equally covered with hair on all sides.

In *Hepoona* and *Phalangista* the grinders are placed in arched series, and they are much larger compared with the size of the skull than in this genus, and the hinder grinders are larger than the front ones ; the front grinder in the upper jaw is larger, more elongate, and compressed.

DACTYLOPSILA TRIVIRGATA.

Dactylopsila trivirgata, Gray, Proc. Zool. Soc. 1858, t. 63.

White ; three broad black stripes on the back, the outer ones commencing on the side of the nose, enclosing the eyes, and continued along the side of the back ; the central one commencing on the crown and continued to the end of the tail, being narrower at the base of the tail : a large black square spot on each side of the chin, separated by a narrow central line ; a large spot on the upper surface of each leg ; the sides of the throat greyish, and the sides

of the body rather greyish from the dark colour of the base of
the fur on that part of the body; the tip of the tail whitish,
and the under part of the upper surface near the tip, with a narrow streak ending some way down the middle of the under side
of the tail, black; the under side of the tip of the tail is bald,
but scarcely callous; the feet flesh-coloured, with few scattered short
whitish hairs; the ears nakedish, black when dry.

Hab. Aru Island (*Wallace*).

a. A female. Aru Island: lives on fruit. "Teeth $\frac{20}{18}$." — *Wallace.*

Order CETE.

Fam. HALICORIDÆ.

HALICORE AUSTRALIS.

Halicore Australis, Owen in Jukes's Voyage of the Fly, ii. 323.
f. 135, 1847; Gray, Voy. Samarang, 33; Fairholme, Proc. Zool.
Soc. 1856, 352.

Hab. Timor Straits.

Order UNGULATA.

Fam. ELEPHANTIDÆ.

SUS PAPUENSIS.   The Bene.

Sus Papuensis, Lesson, Voy. Coquille, t. 8; Müller, Verh. t.   ;
Gray, List Mam. B.M. 185.

Hab. New Guinea (*Lesson*). Called 'Bene.'

a. Adult male. New Guinea. Presented by the Earl of Derby.

List of Mammalia of New Guinea and neighbouring countries.

** indicates that there is a specimen of the species in the Museum for the
locality indicated.

	New Guinea.	Celebes.	Ternate.	Amboyna.	Banda.	Timor.
Macacus Cynomolgos	...	*	...	...	...	*
—— niger	...	**	...	...	...	
Tarsius spectrum	...	*				
Pteropus edulis	...	...	...	...	*	
funereus	...	...	...	**	...	*
phaiops	...	*	...	*	*	
Alecto	...	*				
Chrysoproctus	...	...	...	*		
Macklotii	...	...	...	...	...	**
argentatus	**					
personatus	...	...	*			

TABLE (continued.)

	New Guinea.	Celebes.	Ternate.	Amboyna.	Banda.	Timor.
Pteropus griseus	...	...	...	*	...	**
pallidus	...	...	...	...	*	
Xantharpya amplexicaudata	...	...	...	**	...	**
Cephalotes Peronii	...	...	...	**	*	*
Macroglossus minimus	...	*	...	*	*	*
Harpyia Pallasii	...	*	...	*		
Rhinolophus nobilis	...	...	...	*	...	*
diadema	...	...	...	...	...	*
bicolor	...	...	•••	*	...	*
tricuspidatus	...	...	...	*	...	
euryotis	...	...	...	*		
minor	...	...	...	...	...	*
Hipposideros aurensis	**					
speoris	...	...	...	*	...	*
Mioiopteris Blepotis	...	...	...	*	*	**
Nycticejus Temminckii	...	...	...	...	*	*
Taphozous saccolaimus	...	*	*			
Sorex myosurus	...	...	*	...	*	
tenuis	...	...	...	...	...	*
Felis megalotis	...	...	...	...	...	*
Viverra Zibetha	...	*	...	*		
Paradoxurus musanga	...	...	...	...	...	*
hermaphrodita	**					
Belideus Ariel	**					
Cuscus maculatus	**	...	...	*		
orientalis	**	...	...	*	...	*
ursinus	...	**				
Celebensis	...	**				
Dendrolagus ursinus	**					
inustus	**					
Dorcopsis Asiaticus	**					
Perameles Doreyanus	**					
Phascogale melas	*					
Myoictis Wallacii	**					
Dactylopsila trivirgata	**					
Mus decumanus	...	*	...	*	*	*
Halicore Australis	...	...	...	...	...	**
Sus	...	*	*			
Sus Timorensis	...	...	...	...	...	*
Papuensis	**					
Babirousa alfurus	...	..	*			
Cervus Moluccensis	...	?	*	*	...	*
Kuhlii	...	...	*			
Anoa depressicornis	...	**				

AVES.

FALCONIDÆ.

CUNCUMA LEUCOGASTER.

Falco leucogaster, Gm. S. N. i. p. 257.
Haliaëtus leucogaster, Gould, B. of Austr. pl. 3.
Cuncuma leucogaster, G. R. Gray, List of Accip. p. 24.
Falco blagrus, Müll. Verh. Ethn. p. 21.
Hab. New Guinea ; Lobo (*Müller*) ; Aru Islands (*Wallace*).

HALIASTUR LEUCOSTERNUS, var.

Haliaëtus girrenera, (Vieill.) Less. Voy. Coq. Zool. p. 615.
Haliaëtus leucosternus, Gould, B. of Austr. pl. 4.
Haliastur leucosternus, G. R. Gray, List of B. in B.M. i. p. 13.
Length 17″ ; wings 13″ 3‴.
Hab. New Guinea ; Havre-Dorey (*Less.*) ; Lobo (*Müller*) ; Aru Islands (*Wallace*).
a. Louisiade Archipelago.   Presented by J. Macgillivray, Esq.

BAZA STENOZONA.

Baza stenozoa, G. R. Gray, Proc. Z. S. 1858, p. 169.

Allied to *Baza subcristata*, but is smaller in all its proportions, except in the bill, which is of the same size ; the bands on the under part are narrower, and the rusty colour beneath the body and under wing-coverts is much paler ; the bands on the tail are nearer together, while the one at the tip is broader ; the outer feather on each side differs by being obliquely truncated.
Length 17″ 3‴ ; wings 11″ 9‴.
Hab. Aru Islands (*Wallace*).

ASTUR NOVÆ HOLLANDIÆ.

Falco novæ hollandiæ, Gm. S. N. i. p. 264.
Falco albus, Shaw, Gen. Zool. vii. p. 92.
Astur novæ hollandiæ, Cuv. Règ. An. 1817, i. p. 320.
Astur (*Leucospiza*) *novæ hollandiæ*, Kaup, Classif. der Saüg. und Vög. p. 119.
Hab. New Guinea ; Lobo (*Müller*).

ASTUR LONGICAUDA.

Falco longicauda, Garn. Voy. de la Coq. Zool. i. p. 588.
Hab. New Guinea ; Havre-Dorey (*Garnot*).

ACCIPITER POLIOCEPHALUS.

Accipiter poliocephalus, G. R. Gray, Proc. Z. S. 1858, p. 170.

♀ . Head, back of neck and nape grey ; entire back, wing-coverts

and tail above, plumbeous, the latter with narrow bars of black ;
quills fuscous black ; beneath the body white ; cere and legs red ;
bill and claws black.

Length 14″ 9‴ ; wings 8″ 6‴.

Hab. Aru Islands (*Wallace*).

STRIGIDÆ.

ATHENE HUMERALIS.

Athene humeralis, Pr. B. Consp. Av. p. 40 ; Homb. & Jacq. Voy.
au Pôle Sud, t. 4. f. 1.

Jeraglaux humeralis, Kaup.

Spiloglaux humeralis, Sclater, Proc. L. S. 1858, p. 155.

Rhodoglaux humeralis, Pr. B.

Hab. New Guinea (*Homb. & Jacq.*).

ATHENE THEOMACHA.

Spiloglaux theomacha, Pr. B. Compt. Rend. 1855, p.   .

Hab. New Guinea (*Pr. Bonaparte*).

CAPRIMULGIDÆ.

PODARGUS PAPUENSIS.

Podargus papuensis, Quoy & Gaim. Voy. Astrol. t. 13 ; Gould,
B. of Austr. Suppl. ii. pl. 7.

Hab. New Guinea ; Havre-Dorey (*Quoy & Gaimard*) ; P. Mari-
anne's Straits and Island Aidoema (*Müller*).

PODARGUS OCELLATUS.

Podargus ocellatus, Quoy & Gaim. Voy. Astrol. t. 14.

Hab. New Guinea ; Havre-Dorey (*Quoy & Gaimard*); Aru Islands
(*Wallace*).

CAPRIMULGUS MACRURUS.

Caprimulgus macrurus, Horsf. Linn. Trans. xiii. p. 142 ; Gould,
B. of Austr. ii. pl. 9 ; G. R. Gray, Proc. Z. S. 1858, p. 170.

a. Aru Islands.   Procured from Mr. Wallace.

MACROPTERYX MYSTACEUS.

Cypselus mystaceus, Less. Voy. de la Coqu. t. 22.

Macropteryx mystaceus, Swains. Classif. of B. ii. p. 340.

a. New Guinea (Havre-Dorey).   From the Leyden Museum.

b, c. Aru Islands.   Procured from Mr. Wallace.

COLLOCALIA NIDIFICA, var.

Collocalia nidifica, var., G. R. Gray, Proc. Z. S. 1858, p. 171.

Differs in being rather whiter beneath the body, especially on the
throat.

Collocalia nidifica, G. R. Gray, Gen. of B. i. p. 55.
Hirundo fuciphaga, Thunb.
Hirundo esculenta, var., Lath. Syn. Suppl. pl. 135.
Hirundo brevirostris, McClell.
    a. Chaumont Isle, Louisiade Archipelago. Presented by J. Mac-
gillivray, Esq.

COLLOCALIA HYPOLEUCA.

Collocalia hypoleuca, G. R. Gray, Proc. Z. S. 1858, p. 170.

    Closely allied to *Collocalia Linchi,* Horsf., but is rather larger ;
with the upper surface of a glossy green-black ; side of head, throat
and breast fuscous black, the two latter with the feathers margined
with pure white ; abdomen pure white ; under tail-coverts glossy
green-black.
    ♀. Length 4″ ; wings 4″.
Hab. Aru Islands (*Wallace*).

HIRUNDINIDÆ.

HIRUNDO FRONTALIS.

Hirundo frontalis, Quoy & Gaim. Voy. Astrol. t. 12. f. 1.
Hirundo neoxena, Gould, B. of Austr. pl. 13 ?
Hab. New Guinea ; Havre-Dorey (*Quoy & Gaimard*).

HIRUNDO NIGRICANS.

Hirundo nigricans, Vieill. N. Dict. d'Hist. Nat. xiv. p. 523 ; Voy.
Astrol. t. 12. f. 2.
Collocalia arborea, Gould, B. of Austr. ii. pl. 14.
    a. Aru Islands. Procured from Mr. Wallace.

CORACIADÆ.

EURYSTOMUS PACIFICUS.

Coracias pacifica, Lath. Ind. Orn. Suppl. p. xxvii.
Eurystomus orientalis (L.), Vig. & Horsf.
Eurystomus australis, Swains. ; Gould, B. of Austr. ii. pl. 17.
Eurystomus pacificus, G. R. Gray, Gen. of B. i. p. 62.
Hab. Aru Islands. Procured from Mr. Wallace.

EURYSTOMUS GULARIS.

Eurystomus gularis, Vieill. N. Dict. d'Hist. Nat. xxix. p. 426.
Colaris gularis, Wagl. Syst. Av. Col. sp.
    a. New Guinea. From the Leyden Museum.

CORACIAS PAPUENSIS.

Coracias papuensis, Quoy & Gaim. Voy. Astrol. t. 16.
Coracias Temminckii, Vieill. ?
Hab. New Guinea ; Havre-Dorey (*Quoy & Gaimard*).

PELTOPS BLAINVILLII.

Eurylaimus Blainvillei, Garn. Voy. de la Coqu. t. 19.
Peltops Blainvillei, Wagl.
Hab. New Guinea ; Havre-Dorey (*Garnot*).

ALCEDINIDÆ.

DACELO TYRO.

Dacelo Tyro, G. R. Gray, Proc. Z. S. 1858, pl. 171. pl. 133.

♂. Top, sides of head and back of neck black, spotted and banded with fulvous white ; nape and upper part of back fulvous white, banded and margined with black ; scapulars black ; wing-coverts black, broadly margined with shining blue ; quills and tail black, margined externally with dull blue ; back black, and lower part of back glossy silvery blue ; beneath the body pale fulvous, lighter on throat. Upper mandible black, and lower pale horn-colour.

♀. Quills and tail greenish blue.

Length 13″ ; wings 5¾″.

Juv. Beneath with each feather margined with black ; bill black, tipped with pale horn-colour ; otherwise the same.

a, b. Aru Islands. Procured from Mr. Wallace.

DACELO GAUDICHAUDI.

Alcedo Gaudichaudi, Quoy & Gaim. Voy. Uranie, t. 21.
Chaucalcyon Gaudichaudi, Less.
Dacelo Gaudichaudi, G. R. Gr.

a. New Guinea (Lobo). From Baron Laugier's Collection. Island of Waigiou (*Quoy & Gaimard*).

b, c. Aru Islands. Procured from Mr. Wallace.

DACELO MACRORHINUS.

Dacelo macrorhinus, Less. Voy. de la Coqu. t. 31*. f. 2.
Melidora Euphrosiæ, Less. Tr. d'Orn. p. 249.
Melidora macrorhina, Sclater, Proc. L. S. 1858, p. 156.
Hab. New Guinea ; Havre-Dorey (*Lesson*).

DACELO UNDULATUS.

Alcedo undulata, Scop. Del. Fl. et Fauna Insubr. p. 90 ; Sonn. Voy. N. G. t. 106.
Hab. New Guinea (*Sonnerat*).

HALCYON COLLARIS.

Alcedo collaris, Scop. Del. Flor. et Faun. Insubr. p. 90.
Halcyon collaris, Swains. Zool. Illustr. pl. 27 ; G. R. Gray, Proc. Z. S. 1858, p. 171.
Hab. Aru Islands (*Wallace*).

HALCYON ALBICILLA.

Halcyon albicilla, Less. Tr. d'Orn. p. 247.
Halcyon saurophaga, Gould, Voy. Sulphur, Zool. pl. 19.
a. New Guinea (north coast). Presented by J. Gould, Esq.
b. Louisiade Archipelago. Presented by J. Macgillivray, Esq.

HALCYON SANCTA.

Halcyon sancta, Vig. & Horsf. Linn. Trans. xv. p. 206.
Dacelo chlorocephalus, var. β, Less.
a. Aru Islands. Procured from Mr. Wallace.

HALCYON CINNAMOMINA.

Halcyon cinnamominus, Swains. Zool. Ill. pl. 67.
Hab. New Guinea ; Havre-Dorey (*Lesson*).

HALCYON SORDIDA, var.

Halcyon sordida, var., G. R. Gray, Proc. Z. S. 1858, p. 172.

Rather larger in all its dimensions : length 10″, wings 4″ 2‴,
bill from gape 2″ 5‴ ; but the colour of the back and rump is
brighter than in *Halcyon sordidus,* Gould, B. of Austr. ii. pl. 23.
a. Aru Islands. Procured from Mr. Wallace.
The Hope Isles' specimens measured, length 10″, wings 4″ 6‴,
bill from gape 2″ 9‴ ; while a specimen from Louisiade Archipelago
is of the length of 8″ 6‴, wings 3″ 9‴, and bill from gape 2″ 1‴,
which is about the same size as *H. sordidus,* Gould, but is rather
brighter in its colours, and agrees best with the Aru specimen.

HALCYON TOROTORO.

Syma torotoro, Less. Voy. de la Coqu. t. 31*. f. 1.
Halcyon torotoro, G. R. Gray, Gen. of B. i. p. 79.
Hab. New Guinea ; Havre-Dorey (*Lesson*) ; Lobo (*Müller*) ; Aru
Islands (*Wallace*).

TANYSIPTERA DEA.

Alcedo Dea, Linn. S. N. i. p. 181.
Tanysiptera Dea, Vigors, Linn. Trans. xiv. p. 433.
a. New Guinea (Havre-Dorey). Procured from Baron Laugier's
Collection.
b. New Guinea. Procured from Mr. Turner.

TANYSIPTERA HYDROCHARIS.

Tanysiptera Hydrocharis, G. R. Gray, Proc. Z. S. 1858, p. 172.

Top of head blue ; eyebrows silvery blue ; cheeks, ear-coverts and
nape black ; back and wings deep blue ; rump and beneath the body
white ; middle tail-feathers silvery blue, margined at base, and the
tips white ; lateral tail-feathers black, margined externally with deep
blue. Bill red, and feet fuscous.
Length to end of middle tail-feathers 13″ ; wings 3″ 8‴.

Juv. Rufous brown ; beneath fulvous ; feathers more or less margined with rufous brown.

a–c. Aru Islands. Procured from Mr. Wallace.

CEYX SOLITARIA.

Ceyx solitaria, Temm. Pl. Col. -595. f. 2.
Ceux (Therosa) solitaris, Müll. Verh. Ethn. p. 22.
Ceyx Meninting, Less. Voy. Coqu. Zool. i. p. 691.
Hab. New Guinea ; Lobo (*Müller*) ; Havre-Dorey (*Lesson*) ;
Aru Islands.

CEYX PUSILLA.

Ceyx pusilla, Temm. Pl. Col. 595. f. 3 ; Gould, B. of Austr. ii.
pl. 26.
Hab. New Guinea ; Lobo (*Müller*).
a. Aru Islands. Procured from Mr. Wallace.

ALCYONE AZUREA, var.

Ceyx azurea, Less. Voy. Coqu. Zool. i. p. 690.
Alcyone azurea, var., Gould, B. of Austr. Introd. p. xxxi.
Alcyone pulchra, Gould, Proc. Z. S. 1846, p. 19.
Ceyx Lessonii, Cass. Journ. Acad. Philad. 1850, p. 69.
Hab. New Guinea ; Havre-Dorey (*Lesson*) ; Lobo (*Müller*) ;
Aru Islands (*Wallace*).

UPUPIDÆ.

EPIMACHUS MAXIMUS.

Merops maximus, Scop. Del. Fl. et Fauna Insubr. p. 90 ; Sonn.
Voy. N. G. t. 101.
Upupa magna, Gm. S. N. i. p. 468.
Upupa papuensis, Lath.
Epimachus maximus, Sclater, Proc. L. S. 1858, p. 163.
Epimachus speciosus, G. R. Gray, Gen. of B. i. p. 94.
Epimachus filamentosus, Müll. Verh. Ethn. p. 22.
a. New Guinea. From Baron Laugier's Collection. Lobo
(*Müller*).
b. New Guinea. Procured from Mr. Turner.

EPIMACHUS ALBUS.

Paradisea alba, Blum.
Falcinellus resplendens, Vieill. N. D. d'Hist. Nat. xxviii. p. 165.
Seleucides acanthylis, Less. Hist. Parad. t. 36–38.
Epimachus albus, G. R. Gray, Gen. of B. i. p. 94.
Seleucides albus, Sclater, Proc. L. S. 1858, p. 163.
a. New Guinea. Procured from Baron Laugier's Collection.
b. New Guinea.

EPIMACHUS MAGNIFICUS.

Epimachus magnificus, Cuv. Règ. Anim. 1817, t. 4. f. 2.
Falcinellus magnificus, Vieill. N. D. d'Hist Nat. xxviii. p. 167.
Craspedophora magnifica, G. R. Gray, List. of Gen. of B. 1841,
p. 15.
Ptilorhis magnifica, Gould, B. of Austr. Suppl. pl. .
a. New Guinea. Procured from Baron Laugier's Collection.
b. New Guinea. Procured from Mr. Turner.

PROMEROPIDÆ.

NECTARINIA ASPASIA.

Cinnyris aspasia, Less. Voy. Coqu. t. 30. f. 4.
Cinnyris sericea, Less. Dict. Sci. Nat. iv. p. 21.
Nectarinia aspasia, Müll. Verh. Nat. Gesch. p. 58.
Hab. New Guinea; Havre-Dorey (*Lesson*); Lobo (*Müller*);
Aru Islands (*Wallace*).

NECTARINIA ZENOBIA.

Cinnyris zenobia, Less. Voy. Coqu. t. 30. f. 3.
Cinnyris Clementiæ, Less. Dict. Sci. Nat.
Hab. New Guinea; Havre-Dorey (*Lesson*); Ké Islands (*Wallace*).

NECTARINIA FRENATA.

Nectarinia frenata, Müll. Verh. Nat. Gesch. p. 61. t. 8. f. 1.
Nectarinia australis, Gould, B. of Austr. Suppl. pl. .
Hab. New Guinea (Lobo).
a, b. Aru Islands. Procured from Mr. Wallace.

NECTARINIA EQUES.

Cinnyris eques, Less. Voy. de la Coqu. t. 31.
Phylidonyris eques, Less. Tr. d'Orn. p. 299.
Hab. Island of Waigiou (*Lesson*).

ARACHNOTHERA NOVÆ GUINEÆ.

Cinnyris novæ guineæ, Less. Voy. Coqu. Zool. i. p. 677.
Arachnothera novæ guineæ, Müll. Verh. Nat. Gesch. t. 11. f. 3.
Hab. New Guinea; Havre-Dorey (*Lesson*); Lobo (*Müller*).
a, b. Aru Islands. Procured from Mr. Wallace.

DICÆUM PECTORALE.

Dicæum pectorale, Müll. & Schl. Verh. Ethn. p. 162.
Dicæum erythrothorax, Less. Voy. de la Coqu. t. 30. f. 1?
Hab. New Guinea; Lobo (*Müller*).

DICÆUM IGNICOLLE.

Dicæum ignicolle, G. R. Gr. Proc. Z. S. 1858, p. 173.

♂. Glossy blue-black; under surface olive; middle of abdomen
yellowish white; middle of throat, upper part of breast, and under

tail-feathers vermilion-red, the latter mixed with vermilion-white ; under wing-coverts white.

♂ *juv.* ? Olive ; wings and tail fuscous black ; middle of throat, breast and abdomen yellowish white, with the sides pale olive ; under tail-feathers tinged with vermilion.

Length 3″ 9‴ ; wings 2″ 2‴.

a, b. Aru Islands. Procured from Mr. Wallace.

Allied to *D. hirundinaceum,* but the throat and part of breast are vermilion-red, &c.

PRIONICHILUS NIGER.

Dicæum nigrum, Less. Cent. de Zool. t. 27.
Prionichilus niger, G. R. Gray, Proc. Z. S. 1858, p. 173.
Melanocharis nigra, Sclater, Proc. L. S. 1858, p. 157.
Hab. New Guinea ; Havre-Dorey (*Lesson*) ; Lobo (*Müller*).
a, b. Aru Islands. Procured from Mr. Wallace.

MELIPHAGIDÆ.

MYZOMELA NIGRITA.

Myzomela nigrita, G. R. Gray, Proc. Z. S. 1858, p. 173.

♂. Entirely shining deep black.
♀. Olive-brown, with the front and throat tinged with crimson.
Length 5″ 6‴ ; wings 2″ 3‴.
a, b. Aru Islands. Procured from Mr. Wallace.

MYZOMELA ERYTHROCEPHALA.

Myzomela erythrocephala, Gould, B. of Austr. iv. pl. 64.
a, b. Aru Islands. Procured from Mr. Wallace.

GLYCIPHILA MODESTA.

Glyciphila modesta, G. R. Gray, Proc. Z. S. 1858, p. 174.

♀. Brown, with dashes of dark brown on the feathers ; beneath the body white, with some pale-plumbeous dashes on the sides ; feathers of the breast pale brown, margined broadly with white.
Length 5″ 3‴ ; wings 2″ 6‴.
Hab. Aru Islands (*Wallace*).
A specimen is contained in the British Museum from Goold's Island.

GLYCIPHILA OCULARIS.

Glyciphila ocularis, Gould, B. of Austr. iv. pl. 31.
Hab. New Guinea.
a. Aru Islands. Procured from Mr. Wallace.

PTILOTIS FILIGERA.

Ptilotis filigera, Gould, B. of Austr. Suppl. pl.
a, b. Aru Islands. Procured from Mr. Wallace.

PTILOTIS SIMILIS.

Ptilotis similis, Homb. & Jacq. Voy. Pôle Sud, t. 17. f. 2, 3.
Hab. New Guinea (west coast) (*Homb. & Jacq.*).
a, b. Aru Islands.   Procured from Mr. Wallace.

PTILOTIS MEGARHYNCHUS.

Ptilotis megarhynchus, G. R. Gray, Proc. Z. S. 1858, p. 174.

♂. Brown; top of head olive, with dashes of black in the middle
of each feather; eyes surrounded with yellow; throat yellowish
white, with minute dashes of fuscous; breast and upper part of abdomen fuscous, margined with yellowish olive; sides, abdomen and
under tail-coverts rufous brown; under wing-coverts rufous white.
Length 8″; wings 3″ 6‴; bill 1″ 1‴.
Hab. Aru Islands (*Wallace*).

PTILOTIS FUMATA.

Ptilotis fumata, Müll. (Mus. Lugd.).
Hab. New Guinea; River Oetanata (*Müller*).

PTILOTIS STRIOLATA.   •

Ptilotis striolata, Müll. (Mus. Lugd.).
Hab. New Guinea; River Oetanata (*Müller*).

PTILOTIS AURICULATA.

Ptilotis auriculata, Müll. (Mus. Lugd.).
Hab. New Guinea; Lobo (*Müller*).

TROPIDORHYNCHUS MITRATUS.

Tropidorhynchus corniculatus, Müll. Verh. Ethn. p. 21.
Tropidorhynchus mitratus, Müll.; Sclater, Proc. L. S. vol. ii. p. 158.
Tropidorhynchus buceroides, Gould, B. of Austr. ii. pl. 17?
Hab. New Guinea (west coast); River Oetanata (*Müller*).

TROPIDORHYNCHUS NOVÆ GUINEÆ.

Tropidorhynchus novæ guineæ, Müll. & Schl. Verh. Ethn. p. 153.
Hab. New Guinea (west coast) (*Müller*).
a, b. Aru Islands.   Procured from Mr. Wallace.

TROPIDORHYNCHUS PLUMIGENIS.

Tropidorhynchus plumigenis, G. R. Gray, Proc. Z. S. 1858, p. 174.

♀. Differs from the former by wanting the knob on the basal
part of culmen, and by the sides of the head beneath the eyes being
plumed; the ends of the tail-feathers are margined with brownish
white.

♂ *juv.* Blackish brown; feathers round the base of neck margined with yellow or white.   Probably a younger bird than the
female.
Hab. Ké Island (*Wallace*).

TROPIDORHYNCHUS CHRYSOTIS.

Philedon chrysotis, Less. Voy. de la Coqu. t. 21*.
Myzantha flaviventer, Less. Man. d'Orn. ii. p. 67.
Tropidorhynchus chrysotis, G. R. Gray, Gen. of B. i. p. 125.
Hab. New Guinea ; Havre-Dorey (*Lesson*) ; River Oetanata (*Müller*).

ENTOMOPHILA ALBIGULARIS.

Entomophila albigularis, Gould, B. of Austr. iv. pl. 51.
Hab. New Guinea ; Lobo (*Müller*).

LUSCINIDÆ.

GERYGONE CHRYSOGASTER.

Gerygone chrysogaster, G. R. Gray, Proc. Z. S. 1858, p. 174.

Olive-brown ; stripe from nostrils to eyes, ear-coverts, and sides of neck pale brown ; throat and breast white ; abdomen and under tail-coverts pale yellow. Bill and feet dusky.
Length 4″ 3‴ ; wings 2″ 1‴.
a, b. Aru Islands. Procured from Mr. Wallace.

ZOSTEROPS CITRINELLA.

Zosterops citrinella, Müll. Bp. Consp. Av. p. 398.
Hab. Ké Island (*Wallace*).

ZOSTEROPS GRISEOTINCTA.

Zosterops griseotincta, G. R. Gray, Proc. Z. S. 1858, p. 175.

Yellowish green ; line from each nostril and round each eye white ; quills fuscous black, margined with grey and yellowish green, especially on the tertials. Tail fuscous, tinged with yellowish green ; under surface pale yellow, sides tinged with green and grey.
Length 4″ 7‴ ; wings 2″ 6‴.
a. Louisiade Archipelago. Presented by J. Macgillivray, Esq.
Allied to *Z. luteus*, Gould (B. of Austr. iv. pl. 83) ; but not so rich in colour, being in places tinged with grey.

TURDIDÆ.

EUPETES AJAX.

Eupetes Ajax, Temm. Pl. Col. 573 ; Müll. Verh. Ethn. p. 22.
New Guinea (*Macklot*) ; Lobo (*Müller*).

EUPETES CÆRULESCENS.

Eupetes cærulescens, Temm. Pl. Col. 574 ; Müll. Verh. Ethn. p. 22.
Hab. New Guinea ; Lobo (*Müller*).

BRACHYPTERYX MURINUS.

Myiothera murina, Müll. (Mus. Lugd.).
Turdirostris murina, Pr. B. Consp. Av. p. 218.
Brachypteryx murinus, Sclater, Proc. L. S. 1858, p. 158.
Hab. New Guinea ; Lobo (*Müller*).

ALCIPPE MONACHA.

Alcippe monacha, G. R. Gray, Proc. Z. S. 1858, p. 175.

Castaneous black ; top of head black ; under surface white, with the sides of breast and abdomen obscure brown.

Upper mandible black, and lower one white ; feet pale horn-colour.

Length 4″ 7‴ ; wings 2″ 5‴.

a. Aru Islands.   Procured from Mr. Wallace.

PITTA MACKLOTI.

Pitta Mackloti, Temm. Pl. Col. 547.
Brachyurus Mackloti, Pr. B. Consp. Av. p. 255.
Hab. New Guinea ; Lobo (*Müller*).

a, b. Aru Islands.   Procured from Mr. Wallace.

PITTA NOVÆ GUINEÆ.

Pitta novæ guineæ, Müll. & Schl. Verh. Zool. p. 19.
Pitta atricapilla, Quoy & Gaim. Voy. Astrol. t. 8. f. 3.
Brachyurus novæ guineæ, Pr. B. Consp. Av. p. 256.
Hab. New Guinea ; Havre-Dorey (*Quoy & Gaimard*) ; Lobo (*Müller*).

a, b. Aru Islands.   Procured from Mr. Wallace.

ORIOLUS MÜLLERI.

Oriolus viridissimus, Temm. (Mus. Lugd.).
Mimeta-Mülleri, Pr. B. Consp. Av. p. 346.
Oriolus Mülleri, G. R. Gray, Proc. Z. S. 1858, p. 175.
Hab. New Guinea (*Müller*).

a–c. Aru Islands.   Procured from Mr. Wallace.

ORIOLUS STRIATUS.

Oriolus striatus, Quoy & Gaim. Voy. Astrol. t. 9. f. 2.
Oriolus melanotis, Müll. (Mus. Lugd.).
Mimeta melanotis, Pr. B. Consp. Av. p. 346.

a. New Guinea (Havre-Dorey).   From the Zoological Society's Collection.

ORIOLUS AUREUS.

Oriolus aureus, Linn. S. N. i. p. 163; Le Vaill. Ois. de Parad. t. 18.
Sericulus aureus, Pr. B. Consp. Av. p. 349.
Xanthomelus aureus, Pr. B. Compt. Rend. 1854, p.   .

a. New Guinea.   Procured from Baron Laugier's Collection.

(?) ORIOLUS ANAIS.

Sericulus anais, Less. Rev. Zool. 1839, p. 44.
Melanopyrrhus anais, Pr. B. Compt. Rend. 1854, p.   .
Pastor nigrocinctus, Cassin, Proc. Acad. N. S. of Philad. 1850, p. 68.

Hab. New Guinea (?).

POMATORHINUS ISIDORI.

Pomatorhinus Isidori, Less. Voy. de la Coqu. t. 29. f. 2.
Pomatorhinus Geoffroyi, G. R. Gray, Gen. of B. i. p. 229.
a. New Guinea (Havre-Dorey). Presented by E. Wilson, Esq.
Lobo (*Müller*).

MUSCICAPIDÆ.

MACHÆRIRHYNCHUS XANTHOGENYS.

Machærirhynchus xanthogenys, G. R. Gray, Proc. Z. S. 1858, p. 176.

Differs from *M. flaviventris*, Gould, B. of Austr. Suppl. pl. , by having a rather larger bill, by the back being less green, and the ear-coverts being yellow instead of black.
Length 5″ 3‴; wings 2″ 4‴.
a. Aru Islands. Procured from Mr. Wallace.

MYIAGRA LATIROSTRIS.

Myiagra latirostris, Gould, B. of Austr. ii. pl. 92.
a, b. Aru Islands. Procured from Mr. Wallace.

MYIAGRA LUCIDA.

Myiagra lucida, G. R. Gray, Proc. Z. S. 1858, p. 176.

♂. Black, with the feathers broadly margined with glossy green; quills fuscous black.
Length 7″ 3‴; wings 3″ 9‴.
a. Louisiade Archipelago. Presented by J. Macgillivray, Esq.

PIEZORHYNCHUS RUFOLATERALIS.

Piezorhynchus rufolateralis, G. R. Gray, Proc. Z. S. 1858, p. 176.

Very like *Piezorhynchus nitidus* ♀, Gould (B. of Austr. ii. pl. 88), but the bill is shorter and rather broader at base, which is also furnished with longer and stronger bristles. The sides, under wing-coverts and under tail-coverts pale rusty red; the under surface is also tinged with rusty red.
Length 6″ 9‴; wings 3″ 4‴.
a, b. Aru Islands. Procured from Mr. Wallace.

TODOPSIS CYANOCEPHALA.

♀. *Todus cyanocephalus*, Quoy & Gaim. Voy. Astrol. t. 5. f. 4.
Philentoma cyanocephala, Pucher. Voy. Pôle Sud, t. 20. f. 2.
Todopsis cæruleocephala, Pr. B. Compt. Rend. 1854, p. .
Todopsis cyanocephala, G. R. Gray, Proc. Z. S. 1858, p. 177. pl. 134.

♂. Indigo-blue; front and sides of head deep black; quills and tail black, the latter and tertials margined with blue; beneath, the body deep blue; the tips of the tail slightly margined with white.
Length 6″; wings 2″ 3‴.
Hab. New Guinea; Havre-Dorey (*Quoy & Gaimard*).
a, b. Aru Islands. Procured from Mr. Wallace.

TCHITREA GAIMARDI.

Muscicapa (Tchitrea) Gaimardi, Less. Tr. d'Orn. p. 386.
Hab. New Guinea (*Lesson*).

RHIPIDURA THRENOTHORAX.

Rhipidura threnothorax, Müll. & Schl. Verh. Ethn. p. 185.
Hab. New Guinea ; Lobo (*Müller*).

RHIPIDURA RUFIVENTRIS.

Rhipidura rufiventris, Müll. & Schl. Verh. Ethn. p. 185.
Hab. New Guinea ; Lobo (*Müller*).

RHIPIDURA HYPERYTHRA.

Rhipidura hyperythra, G. R. Gray, Proc. Z. S. 1858, p. 176.

Plumbeous ; head and throat black ; quills and tail fuscous black, margined with plumbeous ; spot at the base of lower mandible, which advances into two lines, one on each side of the throat, and the tips of the wing-coverts and tail-feathers white ; breast and abdomen rusty red ; bill black, lower mandible yellow ; feet dusky olive.
Length 6″ 3‴ ; wings 2″ 9‴.
Hab. Aru Islands (*Wallace*).
This may be the *R. rufiventris,* Müll. ?

RHIPIDURA GULARIS.

Rhipidura gularis, Müll. & Schl. Verh. Ethn. p. 185.
Hab. New Guinea ; Lobo, River Oetanata, and P. Mariannes Straits (*Müller*).

RHIPIDURA ASSIMILIS.

Rhipidura assimilis, G. R. Gray, Proc. Z. S. 1858, p. 176.

Closely allied to *R. isura,* Gould (B. of Austr. ii. pl. 85), but rather larger, with the breast paler ; under wing-coverts buffy white, and the outer tail-feather with less white than in the Australian specimens.
a. Ké Island.   Procured from Mr. Wallace.

RHIPIDURA MACULIPENNIS.

Rhipidura maculipennis, G. R. Gray, Proc. Z. S. 1858, p. 176.

♂. Deep black ; with a line from nostrils passing above the eyes, and a broad line proceeding from the base of the bill on each side of the throat, the tips of the feathers of breast, of tail, of the upper and under wing-coverts, white.
♀. Brownish black ; but similarly marked in other respects with white ; upper mandible and feet black, lower white.
Length 8″ 8‴ ; wings 3″ 2‴.
a, b. Aru Islands.   Procured from Mr. Wallace.

RHIPIDURA ATRIPENNIS.

Rhipidura atripennis, G. R. Gray, Proc. Z. S. 1858, p. 175.

Closely allied to *R. mimoides*, Müll. MSS., but the black is altogether of a deeper hue, while the wings are of a decided black. These differences may be occasioned by the specimens from Aru being more matured.

Length 8″ 9‴; wings 4″.

a, b. Aru Islands. Procured from Mr. Wallace.

MONARCHA INORNATA.

Muscicapa inornata, Garn. Voy. de la Coqu. t. 16. f. 2.
Monarcha inornata, G. R. Gray, Proc. Z. S. 1858, p. 177.
Hab. New Guinea; Havre-Dorey (*Garnot*).

a, b. Aru Islands. Procured from Mr. Wallace.

MONARCHA GUTTULA.

Muscicapa guttula, Garn. Voy. de la Coqu. t. 16. f. 2.
Monarcha guttula, G. R. Gray, Gen. of B. i. p. 260.
Hab. New Guinea; Havre-Dorey (*Garnot*).

a. Aru Islands. Procured from Mr. Wallace.

MONARCHA GRISEOGULARIS.

Monarcha griseogularis, G. R. Gray, Proc. Z. S. 1858, p. 177.

♂. Plumbeous; quills fuscous, slightly margined with grey; some of the tail-coverts and tail deep black; throat plumbeous; ear-coverts and line under each eye black; a line from behind the eye and ending in a spot behind the ear-coverts, abdomen, under tail-coverts, and the tips of the three outer tail-feathers, white; breast mottled with white and pale rust-colour.

Length 6″ 9‴; wings 3″.

a. Aru Islands. Procured from Mr. Wallace.

MONARCHA LEUCURA.

Monarcha leucura, G. R. Gray, Proc. Z. S. 1858, p. 178.

♂. Shining deep black; breast, abdomen and the four outer tail-feathers pure white, with the base of the latter more or less black.

♂ *juv.* Olivaceous plumbeous; top of head greyish plumbeous; middle tail-feathers deep black, the three outer feathers mostly pure white, with the base black; the fourth outer feather black, with white down the shaft and at the tip; chin greyish plumbeous, with a white streak down each feather.

Length 6″ 3‴; wings 3″ 1‴.

a. Ké Island. Procured from Mr. Wallace.

MONARCHA MELANOPTERA.

Monarcha melanoptera, G. R. Gray, Proc. Z. S. 1858, p. 178.

Closely allied to *M. trivirgata*, Temm. (Gould, B. of Austr. ii.

pl. 96), but the black on the forehead, over the eyes and ear-coverts, is posteriorly bordered with white; the wing-coverts deep black.
Length 6″; wings 3″ 3‴.
a. Louisiade Archipelago.   Presented by J. Macgillivray, Esq.

MONARCHA LEUCOTIS.

Monarcha leucotis, Gould, B. of Austr. Suppl. pl.   .
a. Louisiade Archipelago.   Presented by J. Macgillivray, Esq.

MONARCHA TELESCOPHTHALMA.

♂. *Muscicapa telescophthalmus,* Garn. Voy. Coqu. t. 18. f. 1.
Monarcha telescophthalmus, Swains. Classif. of B. ii. p. 257.
Arses telescophthalmus, Less. Tr. d'Orn. p. 387.
♀ or *juv. Muscicapa Enado,* Less. Voy. Coqu. t. 15. f. 2.
Tchitrea Enado, Sclater, Proc. L. S. 1858, p. 161.
a. New Guinea (Havre-Dorey).   From the Leyden Museum.
Lobo (*Müller*).
b, c. Aru Islands.   Procured from Mr. Wallace.

MONARCHA CHRYSOMELA.

♂. *Muscicapa chrysomela,* Garn. Voy. Coqu. t. 18. f. 2.
Monarcha chrysomela, Swains. Classif. of B. ii. p. 257.
Arses chrysomelas, Less. Tr. d'Orn. p. 387.
♀. Yellowish olive; feathers on the head narrowly margined with fuscous; wings and tail fuscous, margined with yellowish olive; throat, breast and sides obscure yellow; abdomen and under tail-coverts deep yellow; spot under each eye pure white.
Hab. New Guinea; Havre-Dorey (*Garnot*); Lobo (*Müller*).
a, b. Aru Islands.   Procured from Mr. Wallace.

MICRŒCA? FLAVOVIRESCENS.

Micrœca flavovirescens, G. R. Gray, Proc. Z. S. 1858, p. 178.

Yellowish green; lore white; wings and tail fuscous, margined with yellowish green; round the eyes and middle of throat, breast, and abdomen yellow; sides pale yellowish green; under tail-coverts yellowish white.   Bill dusky; lower mandible and feet yellow.
Length 5″ 4‴; wings 2″ 11‴.
a, b. Aru Islands.   Procured from Mr. Wallace.

AMPELIDÆ.

PACHYCEPHALA GRISEICEPS.

Pachycephala griseiceps, G. R. Gray, Proc. Z. S. 1858, p. 178.

Olive-brown, tinged with grey on the top of head; line from nostrils extending over each eye, throat and breast white tinged with brown; abdomen and under tail-coverts whitish yellow; wings and tail fuscous, margined with olive.
Length 6″; wings 3″ 3‴.
a. Aru Islands.   Procured from Mr. Wallace.

PACHYCEPHALA RUFIPENNIS.

Pachycephala rufipennis, G. R. Gray, Proc. Z. S. 1858, p. 178.

Olive-brown; line from nostril, extending partly over the eye and throat, brownish white; breast pale rusty brown mixed with white; abdomen white, tinged with yellow; tertials margined with reddish castaneous.

Length 6″ 6‴; wings 3″ 3‴.

a. Ké Island. Procured from Mr. Wallace.

PACHYCEPHALA ? MONACHA.

Pachycephala ? monacha, G. R. Gray, Proc. Z. S. 1858, p. 179.

♂. Head, neck and breast deep black; back, wings and tail fuscous black; abdomen and under tail-coverts white; bill and feet black.

Length 6″ 6‴; wings 3″ 6‴.

a. Aru Islands. Procured from Mr. Wallace.

PACHYCEPHALA LUGUBRIS.

Pachycephala lugubris, Müll. (Mus. Lugd.).
Hab. New Guinea; River Oetanata (*Müller*).

PACHYCEPHALA VIRESCENS.

Pachycephala virescens, Temm. (Mus. Lugd.).
Hab. New Guinea; Lobo (*Müller*).

PACHYCEPHALA SPINICAUDA.

Pachycephala spinicauda, Pucher.Voy. au Pôle Sud, Zool. t. 6. f. 2.
Pucherania spinicaudus, Pr. B. Compt. Rend. 1854, p. .
Hab. Warrior's Island, Torres Straits (*Homb. & Jacq.*).

CAMPEPHAGA PAPUENSIS.

Corvus papuensis, Gm. S. N. i. p. 371.
Graucalus papuensis, Sclater.
Ceblepyris albiventris, Wagl.
Campephaga papuensis, G. R. Gray, Gen. of B. i. p. 283.
Hab. New Guinea; Lobo (*Müller*).

CAMPEPHAGA DESGRAZII.

Graucalus Desgrazii, Pucher. Zool. Pôle Sud, iii. p. 64; Homb. & Jacq. Voy. au Pôle Sud, t. 7. f. 1.
Campephaga Desgrazii, G. R. Gray, Gen. of B. i. p. 283.
Hab. New Guinea (*Homb. & Jacq.*).

CAMPEPHAGA BOYERI.

Campephaga Boyeri, G. R. Gray, Gen. of B. i. p. 283.
Ptiladela Boyeri, Pucher. Zool. Pôle Sud, iii. p. 68.
Hab. New Guinea, west coast (*Homb. & Jacq.*).

CAMPEPHAGA PLUMBEA.

Ceblepyris plumbea, Müll. & Schl. Verh. Ethn. p. 189.
Campephaga plumbea, G. R. Gray, Gén. of B. i. p. 283.
a. New Guinea (River Oetanata).   Presented by E. Wilson, Esq.

CAMPEPHAGA CÆRULEOGRISEA.

Campephaga cæruleogrisea, G. R. Gray, Proc. Z. S. 1858, p. 179.

Closely allied to *Ceblepyris plumbea*, Müll., but larger, and without the rusty yellow on the under-coverts of the tail.
Length 14″ 3‴; wings 6″ 9‴.
Hab. Aru Islands (*Wallace*).

CAMPEPHAGA MELANOPS.

Corvus melanops, Lath. ?
Campephaga melanops, G. R. Gray ; Gould, B. of Austr. ii. pl. 55.
Graucalus melanotis, Gould.
Hab. New Guinea, west coast (*Müller*).
a. Aru Islands.   Procured from Mr. Wallace.

CAMPEPHAGA HYPOLEUCA.

Graucalus hypoleucus, Gould, B. of Austr. ii. pl. 57.
Hab. Aru Islands (*Wallace*).
a. Louisiade Archipelago.   Presented by J. Macgillivray, Esq.

CAMPEPHAGA SCHISTICEPS.

Ceblepyris schisticeps, Pucher. Voy. au Pôle Sud, Zool. iii. p. 70.
t. 10. f. 1.
Campephaga schisticeps, G. R. Gray, Gen. of B. i. p. 283.
Hab. New Guinea, west coast (*Homb. & Jacq.*).

CAMPEPHAGA LARVATA.

Ceblepyris larvata, Müll. & Schl. Verh. Ethn. p. 190.
Campephaga larvata, G. R. Gray, Gen. of B. i. p. 283.
Hab. New Guinea.   Mus. Lugd.

CAMPEPHAGA MELAS.

Ceblepyris melas, Müll. & Schl. Verh. Ethn. p. 189.
Ceblepyris cinnamomea, Müll. & Schl. Verh. Ethn. p. 189.
Edolisoma Marescoti, Pucher. Zool. Pôle Sud, iii. p. 69 ; Voy. au Pôle Sud, t. 10. f. 2.
Edoliisoma melan, Sclater, Proc. L. S. vol. ii. p. 160.
Campephaga melas, G. R. Gray, Gen. of B. i. p. 283.
Hab. New Guinea, west coast (*Homb. & Jacq.*) ; Lobo (*Müller*).

CAMPEPHAGA POLYGRAMMICA.

Campephaga polygrammica, G. R. Gray, Proc. Z. S. 1858, p. 179.

Closely allied to *Campephaga rufiventris* (Puch.), but is more numerously banded on the under surface, which is also of a deeper rusty colour, and there is less white on the wings and at the ends of the tail-feathers.

a. Aru Islands. Procured from Mr. Wallace.

ARTAMUS PAPUENSIS.

Ocypterus papuensis, Temm. ; Bp. Consp. Av. p. 344.
Ocypterus leucorhynchus, Müll. Verh. Nat. Gesch. p. 21.
Hab. New Guinea ; River Oetanata (*Müller*).
a. Aru Islands. Procured from Mr. Wallace.

DICRURUS ASSIMILIS.

Dicrurus assimilis, G. R. Gray, Proc. Z. S. 1858, p. 179.

Closely allied to *Dicrurus bracteatus*, Gould (B. of Austr. ii. pl. 82), but is smaller in all its proportions.
Length 10″ 6‴ ; wings 5″ 4‴.
a, b. Aru Islands. Procured from Mr. Wallace.

DICRURUS MEGALORNIS.

Dicrurus megalornis, G. R. Gray, Proc. Z. S. 1858, p. 179.

Very similar in colouring to the *Dicrurus bracteatus*, but is very much larger in all its proportions.
Length 15″ ; wings 7″ 1‴.
Hab. Ké Island (*Wallace*).

DICRURUS MEGARHYNCHUS.

Edolius megarhynchus, Quoy & Gaim. Voy. Astrol. t. 6.
Dicrurus megarhynchus, G. R. Gray.
Hab. New Guinea ; Havre-Dorey (*Quoy & Gaimard*).

DICRURUS CARBONARIUS.

Dicrourus carbonarius, Pr. B. Consp. Av. p. 352.
Edolius carbonarius, Müll. (Mus. Lugd.).
Hab. New Guinea ; Lobo (*Müller*).

LANIIDÆ.

RECTES KIRROCEPHALUS.

Vanga kirrocephalus, Less. Voy. de la Coqu. t. 11.
Rectes cirrhocephalus, Pr. B. Compt. Rend. xxxi. p. 563.
Timalia poliocephala, Müll. (Mus. Lugd.).
Hab. New Guinea ; Havre-Dorey (*Lesson*).
a. (Lobo.) From the Leyden Museum.

RECTES DICHROUS.

Rectes dichrous, Pr. B. Compt. Rend. xxxi. p. 563.
Garrulus bicolor, Müll. (Mus. Lugd.).
Hab. New Guinea ; Lobo (*Müller*).
a, b. Aru Islands. Procured from Mr. Wallace.

RECTES STREPITANS.

Rectes strepitans, Jacq. & Puch. Voy. Pôle Sud, t. 6. f. 1.
Rectes ferrugineus, Bp. Compt. Rend. xxxi. p. 563.
Hab. New Guinea (west coast) (*Homb. & Jacq.*).
a, b. Aru Islands.   Procured from Mr. Wallace.

MYIOLESTES MEGARHYNCHUS.

Muscicapa megarhyncha, Quoy & Gaim. Voy. Astrol. t. 3. f. 1.
Myiolestes megarhynchus, Müll., Pr. B. Consp. Av. i. p. 358.
Napothera elaeioïdes, Müll. (Mus. Lugd.).
Hab. New Guinea (Havre-Dorey).   From the Leyden Museum.

MYIOLESTES ARUENSIS.

Myiolestes aruensis, G. R. Gray, Proc. Z. S. 1858, p. 180.

Differs from the *M. megarhynchus* by being of an obscure olive-colour, darker on the head; the outer webs of quills greyish brown; and the under surface pale rusty colour, with the throat more inclined to white.
Length 7″ 3‴; wings 3″ 4‴.
♀ similar to the ♂, but with the greater wing-coverts and tertials deep rusty brown.
a. Aru Islands.   Procured from Mr. Wallace.

MYIOLESTES PULVERULENTUS.

Myiolestes pulverulentus, Müll.; Pr. B. Consp. Av. p. 358.
Hab. New Guinea (*Müller*).

CRACTICUS CASSICUS.

✠ *Ramphastos cassicus,* Bodd. Tabl. Pl. Enl. d'Aubent. p. 38.
Coracias varia, Gm. S. N. i. p. 381.
Barita Sonnerati, Less. Tr. d'Orn. p. 346.
Barita varia, Müll. Verh. Ethn. p. 22.
✠ *Cracticus cassicus,* G. R. Gray, Gen. of B. i. p. 300.
Hab. New Guinea (*Auct.*); Lobo (*Müller*).

CRACTICUS PERSONATUS.

Cracticus personatus, Temm. (Mus. Lugd.); Sclater, Proc. L. S. 1858, p. 162; ? G. R. Gray, Proc. Z. S. 1858, p. 180.
Hab. New Guinea; Lobo (*Müller*).
a–c. Aru Islands.   Procured from Mr. Wallace.
These specimens differ from *C. varians* in having the black extending further on the breast, and in having more white at the tips of the outer tail-feathers.

CRACTICUS QUOYI.

Barita Quoyi, Less. Voy. Coqu. t. 14.
Cracticus Quoyi, G. R. Gray, Gen. of B. App. p. 14.
Hab. New Guinea; Havre-Dorey (*Lesson*).
a, b. Aru Islands.   Procured from Mr. Wallace.

CORVIDÆ.

CORVUS ORRU.

Corvus macrorhynchus, pt., Wagl. ?
Corvus orru, Müll. ; Bp. Consp. Av. p. 385.
"Iris sky-blue" (*Wallace*).
Hab. New Guinea ; Havre-Dorey (*Müller*).
a, b. Aru Islands. Procured from Mr. Wallace.

CORVUS CORONOIDES?

Corvus corone, p., Wagl. Syst. Av. Corv. sp. 6.
Hab. New Guinea (*Wagler*).

GYMNOCORVUS SENEX.

Corvus senex, Less. Voy. de la Coqu. t. 24.
Gymnocorvus tristis, Less. Tr. d'Orn. p. 327.
Gymnocorvus senex, G. R. Gray, Gen. of B. ii. p. 315.
Hab. New Guinea ; Havre-Dorey (*Lesson*).

PARADISEIDÆ.

PARADISEA APODA.

Paradisea apoda, Linn. S. N. i. p. 166.
a. New Guinea.
b. New Guinea. Presented by J. B. Kingdom, Esq.
c. New Guinea. From the Zoological Society's Collection.

Var. *Wallaciana*.

Paradisea apoda, var. *Wallaciana*, G. R. Gray, Proc. Z. S. 1858, p. 181.
Paradisea apoda, Less. Voy. de la Coqu. i. p. 526.

The "intensely shining orange-coloured" lateral plumes easily distinguish this bird from the specimens of *P. apoda* in the British Museum, and from the representations given in the works of Le-vaillant, Vieillot, and Lesson, &c. The yellow on the top of the head and back of neck is also of a much paler colour, both in the specimens with and without lateral plumes. In Forrest's 'Voyage to New Guinea' it is stated that the Great Bird of Paradise of Aroo migrated, "when the easterly or wet monsoon set in," to New Guinea ; but we learn from the interesting paper * of Mr. A. R. Wallace that this "is quite incorrect, as they are permanent resi-dents in Aru, and the natives know nothing of their being found in New Guinea." The two differences previously mentioned, which were uniform in all the specimens sent home by Mr. Wallace, induce me to suppose that, if not a *distinct* species, it is at least a well-marked local variety of the Great Bird of Paradise.
a–c. Aru Islands. Procured from Mr. Wallace.

* Ann. and Mag. of Nat. Hist. 1857, vol. xx. p. 411.

PARADISEA PAPUANA.

Paradisea papuana, Less. Voy. de la Coqu. Zool. i. p. 446.

a. New Guinea (Havre-Dorey). From the Zoological Society's Collection. River Oetanata ; Lobo (*Müller*).

PARADISEA REGIA.

Paradisea regia, Linn. S. N. i. p. 166.
Cicinnurus spiniturnix, Less.
Cicinnurus regius, Pr. B.

a. New Guinea ; Havre-Dorey. Procured from Mr. Turner. Lobo ; River Oetanata (*Müller*).

b–d. Aru Islands. Procured from Mr. Wallace.

PARADISEA ATRA.

Paradisea atra, Bodd. Tabl. Pl. Enl. d'Aubent. p.38; Pl. Enl. 632.
Paradisea superba, Scop. Del. Fl. et Fauna Insubr. p. 88 ; Sonn. Voy. N. G. t. 96.
Lophorina atra, Sclater.

a. New Guinea (Havre-Dorey). Procured from Mr. Turner.

PARADISEA SPECIOSA.

Paradisea speciosa, Bodd. Tabl. Pl. Enl. d'Aubent. p. 38; Pl. Enl. 631.
Paradisea magnifica, Scop. Del. Fl. et Fauna Insubr. p. 88 ; Sonn. Voy. N. G. t. 98.

a. New Guinea (Havre-Dorey). Procured from Mr. Turner.

PARADISEA SEXPENNIS.

Paradisea sexpennis, Bodd. Tabl. Pl. Enl. d'Aubent. p. 39 ; Pl. Enl. 633.
Oriolus aureus, Gm. S. N. i. p. 163.
Parotia aurea, Less.

a. New Guinea. Procured from Mr. Turner.
b. New Guinea. Procured from Mr. Wakeham.

PARADISEA RUBRA.

Paradisea rubra, Vieill.

a, b. Island Waigiou. From Baron Laugier's Collection.
c. New Guinea ? Procured from Mr. Turner.

(?) PARADISEA WILSONI.

Lophorina respublica, Pr. B. Compt. Rend. 1850, p. 131.
Diphyllodes respublica, Pr. B. Consp. Av. p. 431.
Paradisea Wilsoni, Cassin, Proc. Acad. N. S. of Philad. 1850, p. 57 ; Journ. Acad. N. S. of Philad. ii. pl. 15.
Diphyllodes Wilsoni, Sclater.
Hab. New Guinea (?).

ASTRAPIA NIGRA.

Paradisea nigra, Gm. S. N. i. p. 401.

Paradisea gularis, Lath.
Astrapia gularis, Vieill. Gal. des Ois. t. 107.
a. New Guinea. From Baron Laugier's Collection.
b, c. New Guinea. Procured from Mr. Turner.

ASTRAPIA CARUNCULATA.

Paradigalla carunculata, Less. Rev. de Zool. 1840, p. 1 ; Voy.
de la Bonite, t. 1.
Hab. New Guinea (*Lesson*).

STURNIDÆ.

PTILONORHYNCHUS BUCCOIDES.

Kitta buccoides, Temm. Pl. Col. 575.
Ptilonorhynchus buccoides, G. R. Gray.
Hab. New Guinea ; Lobo (*Müller*).

PTILONORHYNCHUS MELANOTIS.

Ptilonorhynchus melanotis, G. R. Gray, Proc. Z. S. 1858, p. 181.

Head, neck and nape fulvous white margined with black, and
on the latter with green ; back, wings, and upper side of tail green ;
tips of some of the wing-coverts, of tertials and of tail-feathers buffy
white ; throat white, narrowly margined with black ; under surface
fulvous white, tinged in some places with yellow and pale green, and
margined with black on breast, fore part of abdomen, and sides ;
under wing- and tail-coverts buffy white ; bill yellow, and feet plumbeous.
Length 13″ 6‴ ; wings 7″.
a. Aru Islands. Procured from Mr. Wallace.

MANUCODIA CHALYBEA.

Manucodia chalybea, Bodd. Tabl. Pl. Enl. d'Aubent. p. 39.
Paradisea viridis, Scop. Del. Fl. et Fauna Insubr. p. 88 ; Sonn.
Voy. N. G. t. 100.
Phonygama viridis, G. R. Gray, Gen. of B. ii. p. 303.
a. New Guinea (Havre-Dorey). From Baron Laugier' Collection.
b, c. Aru Islands. Procured from Mr. Wallace.

MANUCODIA ATRA.

Phonygama atra, Less. Voy. de la Coqu. Zool. i. p. 639.
Manucodia atra, Sclater, Proc. L. S. 1858, p. 162.
Hab. New Guinea ; Havre-Dorey (*Lesson*).

MANUCODIA KERAUDRENI.

Barita Keraudreni, Less. Voy. de la Coqu. t. 13.
Chalybæus cornutus, Cuv. Règ. An. 1817, i. p. .

Phonygama Lessonia, Swains. Classif. of B. ii. p. 264.
Manucodia Keraudreni, Sclater.
Hab. New Guinea ; Havre-Dorey (*Lesson*).

CALORNIS VIRESCENS.

Calornis virescens, G. R. Gray, Proc. Z. S. 1858, p. 182.
Lamprotornis cantor, Müll. Verh. Ethn. p. 21 ?

Differs from *L. metallicus* (Temm.) in having the purple glossy
appearances only on the head, nape, and upper part of breast ; in
these respects it agrees with the specimen (*C. nitida*) from New
Ireland, but the latter is rather larger in all its dimensions ; and it
is also similar in colour to the specimen (*C. amboinensis*) from Amboyna, while in this the bill is rather larger and more arched than
either of the others, and the tail and wings are rather less in length
than in the New Ireland species.
Length 8″ 9‴ to the end of middle tail-feathers ; wings 4″ 2‴.
a–d. Aru Islands.   Procured from Mr. Wallace.
Hab. New Guinea ; Lobo (*Müller* ?).

GRACULA DUMONTII.

Mino Dumontii, Less. Voy. de la Coqu. t. 25.
Gracula Dumontii, Wagl.
a. New Guinea (Havre-Dorey).   From the Zoological Society's
Collection.   Lobo (*Müller*).
b, c. Aru Islands.   Procured from Mr. Wallace.

BUCERIDÆ.

BUCEROS RUFICOLLIS.

Buceros ruficollis, Vieill. ; Temm. Pl. Col. 557.
Buceros plicatus, Less. Tr. d'Orn. p. 445.
Hab. New Guinea ; Havre-Dorey (*Lesson*) ; Lobo (*Müller*) ;
Island of Waigiou (*Temminck*).

PSITTACIDÆ.

PLATYCERCUS AMBOINENSIS.

Psittacus amboinensis, Bodd. Tabl. Pl. Enl. d'Aubent. p. 14 ;
Pl. Enl. 240.
Psittacus dorsalis, Quoy & Gaim. Voy. Astrol. t. 21. f. 2.
Platycercus amboinensis, Wagl. Monogr. Psitt. p. 539.
Aprosmictus amboinensis, Pr. B. Rev. et Mag. de Zool. 1854, p. 153.
a. New Guinea (Havre-Dorey).   From Baron Laugier's Collection.
Lobo (*Müller*).

? PLATYCERCUS NOVÆ GUINEÆ.

Cyanorhamphus novæ guineæ, Pr. B. Cab. Journ. für Ornith.
1856, p.   .
Hab. New Guinea ? (*Pr. Bonaparte*).

CHARMOSYNA PAPUENSIS.

Psittacus papou, Scop. Del. Fl. et Fauna Insubr. p. 86 ; Sonn.
Voy. N. G. t. 111.
Psittacus papuensis, Gm. S. N. i. p. 317.
Charmosyna papuensis, Wagl.
a. New Guinea (Havre-Dorey).   Procured from Mr. Turner.
b. New Guinea.

LORIUS DOMICELLA.

Psittacus domicella, Linn. S. N. i. p. 145.
Domicella atricapilla, Wagl. Monogr. Psitt. p. 567.
Lorius domicella, Vigors.
Hab. New Guinea ; Havre-Dorey (*Lesson*).

LORIUS TRICOLOR.

Psittacus Lory, Linn. S. N. i. p. 145.
Lorius tricolor, Steph. Gen. Zool.
Hab. New Guinea ; Havre-Dorey (*Lesson*).

LORIUS HYPOINOCHROUS.

Lorius hypoinochrous, G. R. Gray, List of Psitt. p. 49.
a. Louisiade Archipelago.   Presented by J. Macgillivray, Esq.

LORIUS CARDINALIS.

Psittacus cardinalis, Bodd. Tabl. Pl. Enl. d'Aubent. p. 30.
Psittacus puniceus, Gm. S. N. i. p. 335.
Domicella punicea, Wagl. Monogr. Psitt. p. 569.
Hab. New Guinea (*Wagler*).

EOS SQUAMATA.

Psittacus squamatus, Bodd. Tabl. Pl. Enl. d'Aubent. p. 42 ; Pl.
Enl. 684.
Psittacus guebiensis, Gm. S. N. i. p. 318.
Eos guebiensis, Wagl. Monogr. Psitt. p. 559.
Eos squamata, G. R. Gray, Gen. of B. ii. p. 417.
Hab. New Guinea ; Havre-Dorey (*Lesson*).

EOS SCINTILLATA.

Psittacus scintillans, Temm. Pl. Col. 569.
Eos scintillata, G. R. Gray, Gen. of B. ii. p. 417.
Chalcopsitta scintillata, Pr.B. Rev. et Mag. de Zool. 1854, p. 156.
Hab. New Guinea (Lobo).

EOS RUBRIFRONS.

Chalcopsitta rubrifrons, G. R. Gray, Proc. Z. S. 1858, p. 182.
pl. 135.

The front, lores, sides of the breast, and spots on throat carmine ;
hind head and ear-coverts purplish black ; throat purple with streaks

of green ; breast purplish green, with a broad orange-yellow streak down the shaft of each feather ; back of neck and nape purplish green, streaked down the shafts with rich yellow ; scapulars, wings and tail green ; back and rump light green streaked with yellow ; under wing-coverts, inner webs near the base of tail, and thighs, carmine ; quills beneath at base yellow, tinged on some feathers with carmine ; abdomen, sides, and under tail-coverts green, streaked with yellow intermixed near the thighs with crimson ; beneath the tail carmine, tipped with obscure yellow.

Length 12″ ; wings 7″ 2‴.

a, b. Aru Islands.   Procured from Mr. Wallace.

Allied to *C. scintillata,* which has the ends of the tail-feathers acutely pointed, while in the Aru species they are decidedly rounded.

Eos RUBIGINOSA.

Chalcopsitta rubiginosa, Pr. B. Proc. Z. S. 1850, p. 26. pl. xvi.
a. Island of Waigiou.   Procured from M. Verreaux.

Eos ATRA.

Psittacus ater, Scop. Del. Fl. et Fauna Insubr. p. 87 ; Sonn. Voy. N. G. t. 110.
Psittacus novæ guineæ, Gm. S. N. i. p. 319.
Chalcopsitta atra, Pr. B.
Hab. New Guinea (*Sonnerat*).

Eclectus POLYCHLOROS.

Psittacus polychloros, Scop. Del. Fl. et Fauna Insubr. p. 87.
Hab. New Guinea.   Island of Waigiou.

Var. *aruensis.*

Psittacus magnus, pt., Wagl.

This variety differs from the *E. polychloros* by having the ends of the tail-feathers above more prominently tipped with yellow, which is in some feathers tinged with purple.

a. Aru Islands.   Procured from Mr. Wallace.

Eclectus LINNÆI.

Eclectus Linnæi, Wagl. Monogr. Psitt. p. 571. t. 22.
Eclectus puniceus, Pr. B. Rev. et Mag. de Zool. 1854, p. 155.
Eclectus grandis, Müll. Verh. Ethn. p. 22.
Eclectus cardinalis, Sclat. ?
Hab. New Guinea ; Havre-Dorey (*Lesson*) ; Lobo (*Müller*).
a. Aru Islands.   Procured from Mr. Wallace.

Eclectus PARAGUANUS.

Psittacus paraguanus, Gm. S. N. i. p. 336.
Psittacodis Paraguæ, Wagl. Monogr. Psitt. p. 574. t. 33.
Psittacus Stavorini, Less. Voy. de la Coqu. Zool. p. 628.
Hab. Island of Waigiou (*Lesson*).

ECLECTUS ? TARABE.

Psittacus Taraba, Gm. S. N. i. p. 344.
Psittacodis Tarabe, Wagl. Monogr. Psitt. p. 577.
Hab. New Guinea? (*Wagler*).

TRICHOGLOSSUS CYANOGRAMMUS.

Psittacus hæmatodus, Bodd. Tabl. Pl. Enl. d'Aubent. p. 4 ; Pl. Enl. 61.
Trichoglossus cyanogrammus, Wagl. Monogr. Psitt. p. 554.
a. New Guinea (west coast).

TRICHOGLOSSUS NIGROGULARIS.

Trichoglossus nigrogularis, G. R. Gray, Proc. Z. S. 1858, p. 183.
Trichoglossus capistratus, var., Müll.?

Green; front and sides of the head azure; occiput dark bronzy green; semicollar above greenish yellow; throat blue-black; nape scarlet broadly margined with green; breast tinged with yellow narrowly margined with black; abdomen green broadly margined with black; fore part of sides scarlet bordered with green; hind part of sides, thighs and under tail-coverts yellow bordered with green; under wing-coverts scarlet; quills black beneath and yellow at their bases.

Length 13″ 6‴ ; wings 6″ 3‴.
Hab. New Guinea?
a, b. Aru Islands. Procured from Mr. Wallace.
It is intermediate between *T. Swainsoni* and *T. cyanogrammus*.

TRICHOGLOSSUS COCCINEIFRONS.

Trichoglossus coccineifrons, G. R. Gray, Proc. Z. S. 1858, p. 183.

Green; front and spots on the head carmine; head and chin whitish blue; nape and upper part of the abdomen scarlet, the two latter margined with blue; some of the lesser wing-coverts marked with yellow and scarlet; under wing-coverts and inner margins of tail-feathers scarlet; base of quills beneath yellow tinged with scarlet, quills above green marked in some places with yellow; abdomen varied with blue, green, scarlet and yellow; under tail-coverts varied with yellow, green and pale scarlet.

Length 11″; wings 5″ 10‴.
Hab. Aru Islands (*Wallace*).

CORIPHILUS PLACENTIS.

Psittacus placentis, Temm. Pl. Col. 553.
Coriphilus placentis, G. R. Gray, Gen. of B. ii. p. 417.
Psitteuteles placens, Pr. B. Rev. et Mag. de Zool. 1854, p. 157.
Trichoglossus placens, Sclater, Proc. L. S. 1858, p. 164.
a, b. New Guinea (River Oetanata). From the Leyden Museum.
Aru Islands (*Wallace*).

PSITTACUS PERSONATUS.

Psittacus batavensis, Lath. Ind. Orn. i. p. 126?
Psittacus Geoffroyi, Kuhl, Consp. Psitt. p. 85.
Geoffroyus personatus, Pr. B. Rev. et Mag. de Zool. 1854, p. 155.
Hab. New Guinea; Lobo (*Müller*).

PSITTACUS PUCHERANI.

Pionus fuscicapillus, Homb. & Jacq. Voy. au Pôle Sud, t. 25*. f. 3.
Geoffroius Pucherani, Pr. B.
Hab. New Guinea, west coast (*Homb. & Jacq.*).

PSITTACUS ARUENSIS.

Psittacus aruensis, G. R. Gray, Proc. Z. S. 1858, p. 183.

♂. Green, paler on the margins of the feathers; top of head silvery blue; front and cheeks scarlet-red; chin reddish yellow; under surface yellowish green; spot on each wing castaneous red; under wing-coverts verditer blue.

♀. Head rusty brown; otherwise yellowish green.

♂ juv. Head of the same green as the back, but the sides of head brownish green.

Length 8″ 9‴; wings 6″ 3‴.

a, b. Aru Islands. Procured from Mr. Wallace.

PSITTACUS CAPISTRATUS.

Psittacus capistratus, G. R. Gray, Proc. Z. S. 1858, p. 183.

♂. Head brown tinged with green, and mixed with dull rufous; general colour green edged with paler; upper tail-coverts yellowish green; under wing-coverts and the fore part of the sides verditer blue.

Like the female of the preceding species, but it is much larger in size.

Length 12″; wings 7″ 5‴.

a. Ké Islands. Procured from Mr. Wallace.

PSITTACULA DESMARESTI.

Psittacus Desmaresti, Garn. Voy. de la Coqu. t. 35.
Psittacula (Psittaculirostris) Desmaresti, Less. Tr. d'Orn. p. 204.
Cyclopsitta Desmaresti, Pr. B. Rev. et Mag. de Zool. 1854, p. 154.
Hab. New Guinea; Havre-Dorey (*Garnot*); Lobo (*Müller*).

PSITTACULA DIOPHTHALMA.

Cyclopsitta diophthalma, Homb. & Jacq. Voy. Pôle Sud, t. 25 *bis,* f. 4, 5.
Psittacula diophthalma, Homb. & Jacq.
Hab. New Guinea, south coast (*Homb. & Jacq.*).
a, b. Aru Islands. Procured from Mr. Wallace.

NASITERNA PYGMÆA.

Psittacus pygmæus, Quoy & Gaim. Voy. Astrol. t. 21.
Micropsitta pygmæa, Less. Tr. d'Orn. p. 646.

Nasiterna pygmæa, Wagl. Monogr. Psitt. p. 631.
Hab. New Guinea; Havre-Dorey (*Quoy & Gaimard*); River Oetanata (*Müller*).

CACATUA TRITON.

Cacatua triton, Temm. Consp. Gen. Ind. Arch. iii. p. 405.
Psittacus galeritus, Less. Voy. Coqu. Zool. i. p. 624 ?
Cacatua cyanopis, Bl. Journ. A. S. B. 1856, p. 447.
Length 16″; wings 10″ 3‴.
Hab. New Guinea; Havre-Dorey (*Lesson*); west coast (*Müller*).
a. Aru Islands. Procured from Mr. Wallace.

CACATUA ÆQUATORIALIS.

Cacatua æquatorialis, Temm. Coup d'œil, &c. i. p. 405.
Cacatua sulphurea, Less. Voy. de la Coqu. i. p. 626.
Hab. New Guinea; Havre-Dorey (*Lesson*).

MICROGLOSSUM ATERRIMUM.

Psittacus aterrimum, Gmel. S. N. i. p. 330.
Psittacus gigas, Lath.
Psittacus (*Prosciger*) *aterrimus*, Kuhl, Consp. Psitt. pp. 22, 91.
Psittacus griseus, Bechst.
Microglossum aterrimum, Wagl. Monogr. Psitt. p. 682.
Hab. New Guinea (Havre-Dorey); Island of Waigiou (*Lesson*); Lobo (*Müller*).
a, b. Aru Islands. Procured from Mr. Wallace.

MICROGLOSSUM ALECTO.

Microglossum Alecto, Temm.; Pr. B. Consp. Av. p. 7.
Hab. New Guinea (*Temminck*).

DASYPTILUS PECQUETII.

Psittacus Pecquetii, Less. Bull. Univ. 1831, p. 241; Illustr. de Zool. t. 1.
Dasyptilus Pecquetii, Wagl. Monogr. Psitt. p. 681.
Hab. New Guinea? (*Lesson*).

CUCULIDÆ.

CENTROPUS MENEBIKI.

Centropus Menebiki, Garn. Voy. Coqu. t. 33.
Hab. New Guinea; Havre-Dorey (*Garnot*); Lobo (*Müller*).
a. Aru Islands. Procured from Mr. Wallace.

CENTROPUS SPILOPTERUS.

Centropus spilopterus, G. R. Gray, Proc. Z. S. 1858, p. 184.

Greenish bronzy black ; shafts of the feathers strong and deep
shining black ; wings with small irregular spots of brownish white.
Length 21″ ; wings 9″ 3‴.
Hab. Ké Islands (*Wallace*).

EUDYNAMYS PUNCTATUS.

Cuculus rufiventris, Less. Voy. de la Coqu. Zool. i. p. 623.
Eudynamys rufiventris, G. R. Gray, Gen. of B. ii. p. 464.
Eudynamys punctatus, Pr. B. Consp. Gen. Av. i. p. 101.
Hab. New Guinea ; Havre-Dorey (*Lesson*).

CUCULUS LEUCOLOPHUS.

Hierococcyx leucolophus, Müll. & Schl. Verh. Ethn. pp. 22, 233.
Hab. New Guinea ; Lobo (*Müller*).

CUCULUS ASSIMILIS.

Cuculus assimilis, G. R. Gray, Proc. Z. S. 1858, p. 184.

Allied to *C. flavus.* Bronzy brown, marked on some of the edges
with pale rufous ; side of head and chin tinged with grey ; under surface rusty colour, with the throat, breast and abdomen banded with
slate-colour ; tail bronzy brown, with triangular marks along the
edges of each feather.
Hab. Aru Islands (*Wallace*).

CUCULUS MEGARHYNCHUS.

Cuculus megarhynchus, G. R. Gray, Proc. Z. S. 1858, p. 184.

Top and sides of the head greyish black ; upper surface bronzy
brown edged with rusty ; under surface brownish white mixed with
rusty, and spotted with minute spots of greyish black ; tail bronzy
brown, tipped with rusty white, with the outer feather banded in the
inner web with rusty white.
Length 7″ 6‴ ; wings 3″ 9‴.
Hab. Aru Islands (*Wallace*).

CHRYSOCOCCYX LUCIDUS.

Cuculus lucidus, Gm. S. N. i. p. 421.
Chrysococcyx lucidus, Gould, B. of Austr. iv. pl. 88.
Hab. New Guinea ; Lobo (*Müller*).

COLUMBIDÆ.

PTILONOPUS PULCHELLUS.

Columba pulchella, Temm. Pl. Col. 564.
Ptilonopus pulchellus, G. R. Gray, Gen. of B. ii. p. 466.
a. New Guinea. Procured from Mr. Cuming. Lobo (*Müller*).

PTILONOPUS WALLACII.

Ptilonopus Wallacii, G. R. Gray, Proc. Z. S. 1858, p. 183. pl. 136.

Top of head carmine ; cheeks and throat pure white ; neck, nape and breast greyish white ; lower part of breast with a band of white bordered posteriorly with a broad one of orange ; lesser wing-coverts with a band of deep orange ; abdomen and under tail-coverts varied with yellow and green ; upper part of back orange-green ; scapulars and some of the greater wing-coverts grey margined with orange-yellow ; the other greater wing-coverts and secondaries yellowish green margined with yellow ; quills rich emerald-green ; tertials yellowish green spotted with grey ; lower part of back rich yellowish green ; tail coppery green with the apical half greenish white ; bill yellow, and feet red.

Length 10″ ; wings 5″ 9‴.

a, b. Aru Islands.   Procured from Mr. Wallace.

Most allied to *Ptilonopus pulchellus*, but differs in several respects.

PTILONOPUS AURANTIIFRONS.

Ptilonopus aurantiifrons, G. R. Gray, Proc. Z. S. 1858, p. 185. pl. 137.

Front deep rich orange ; occiput and sides of head yellowish green ; chin pure white ; neck sooty grey ; breast and beneath the body yellowish green mixed with grey on the thighs ; nape and scapulars grey, each feather of former margined with orange, those of the latter margined with green ; back and wing-coverts green, with some of the feathers spotted with grey, and others margined with orange-yellow ; quills rich emerald-green with the secondaries bordered with yellow ; tail coppery green with a narrow band of grey at the tip, which is white beneath ; under tail-coverts yellow varied with green ; bill yellow ; cere and feet red.   " Iris orange."

Length 9″ 9‴ ; wings 5″ 6‴.

a, b. Aru Islands.   Procured from Mr. Wallace.

PTILONOPUS CORONULATUS.

Ptilonopus coronulatus, G. R. Gray, Proc. Z. S. 1858, p. 185. pl. 138.

Yellowish green ; front whitish purple, with posteriorly a narrow band of purple, and then a broader band of golden yellow ; occiput deep green ; chin yellowish white ; wings and tail shining emerald-green margined narrowly with yellow ; a spot on fore part of abdomen purple ; middle of hind part of abdomen and under tail-coverts bright yellow.

Length 7″ 9‴ ; wings 4″ 6‴.   Iris orange.

a. Aru Islands.   Procured from Mr. Wallace.

PTILONOPUS VIRIDIS.

Columba viridis, Linn. S. N. i. p. 283 ; Pl. Enl. 142.

Ptilinopus viridis, Swains. Zool. Journ. i. p. 473.
Iotreron viridis, Pr. B. Consp. Av. ii. p. 24.
Hab. New Guinea ; Lobo (*Müller*).

PTILONOPUS STROPHIUM.

Columba Rivolii, Knip & Prev. t. 17 ?
Ptilonopus Strophium, Gould, Jard. Contr. of Orn. 1850, p. 105.
Iotreron Rivolii, p., Pr. B. Consp. Av. ii. p. 25.
a. Louisiade Archipelago.　Presented by Mr. Macgillivray.
b. Louisiade Archipelago.　Procured from M. Verreaux.

PTILONOPUS PRASINORRHOUS.

Ptilonopus prasinorrhous, G. R. Gray, Proc. Z. S. 1858, p. 185.

Closely allied to *Ptilonopus Rivoli*, but it is at once distinguished
by the vent and under tail-coverts being green, slightly margined
on each feather with yellow ; the reddish-purple patch on the abdomen is connected to the white pectoral band ; bill yellow, and feet
red.
a. Ké Islands.　Procured from Mr. Wallace.

PTILONOPUS NANUS.

Columba naina, Temm. Pl. Col. 565.
Ptilonopus naina, G. R. Gray, Gen. of B. ii. p. 467.
Ptilopus nanus, Pr. B.
Iotreron nana, Pr. B. Consp. Av. ii. p. 25.
Hab. New Guinea ; Lobo (*Müller*).

PTILONOPUS IOZONUS.

Ptilonopus iozonus, G. R. Gray, Proc. Z. S. 1858, p. 186.

♂. Yellowish green ; bend of wings greyish violet mixed with
green ; middle of the abdomen deep orange; vent and under tail-
coverts white varied with yellow; greater wing-coverts and tertials
bordered with yellow, the latter grey in the middle of each feather ;
quills shining deep emerald-green ; under surface of wings slate-colour; tail green with a broad band of grey at the tip, which is
white beneath, especially on the inner webs.
♀. With a patch on the abdomen of an orange-yellow.
Length 8″ 3‴ ; wings 4″ 9‴.
a. Aru Islands.　Procured from Mr. Wallace.
Most like *Ptilonopus nanus*.

PTILONOPUS SUPERBUS.

Columba superba, Temm. Pig. t. 33.
Ptilonopus superbus, Steph. Gen. Zool. xiv. 1. p. 279 ; Gould, B.
of Austr. v. pl. 57.
Lamprotreron superba, Bp. Consp. Av. ii. p. 18.
Hab. New Guinea ; Lobo (*Müller*).
a. Aru Islands.　Procured from Mr. Wallace.

PTILONOPUS PERLATUS.

Columba perlata, Temm. Pl. Col. 559.
Ptilonopus perlatus, G. R. Gray, Gen. of B. ii. p. 466.
Sylphitreron perlatus, Verr. ; Bp. Consp. Av. ii. p. 40.
Hab. New Guinea; Lobo (*Müller*).
a. Aru Islands.   Procured from Mr. Wallace.

PTILONOPUS CYANOVIRENS.

Columba cyanovirens, Less. Voy. de la Coqu. t. 42. f. 1.
Ptilinopus cyanovirens, Selby, Nat. Libr. v. p. 109. pl. 5.
Ptilonopus leucogaster, Swains. Classif. of B. ii. p. 347.
Cyanotreron cyanovirens, Pr. B. Consp. Av. ii. p. 23.
Hab. New Guinea ; Havre-Dorey (*Lesson*).

CARPOPHAGA CHALYBURA.

Carpophaga chalybura, Bp. Consp. Av. ii. p. 32.
Columba ænea, ♂ , Temm. Pig. t. 3.
Columba ænea, var. β, Wagl. Syst. Av. Col. sp. 15.
a. Aru Islands.   Procured from Mr. Wallace.

CARPOPHAGA SUNDEVALII.

Globicera Sundevalii, Pr. B. Consp. Av. ii. p. 32.
Carpophaga Sundevalii, G. R. Gray, List of Col. B.M. p. 18.
a. Island of Waigiou.   Procured from M. Verreaux.
b–d. Louisiade Archipelago.   Presented by Mr. Macgillivray.

? CARPOPHAGA MYRISTICIVORA.

Columba myristicivora, Scop. Del. Fl. et Fauna Insubr. p. 94 ;
Sonn. Voy. N. G. t. 102.
Carpophaga myristicivora, G. R. Gray, Gen. of B. ii. p. 468.
Hab. New Guinea (*Sonnerat*).

? CARPOPHAGA BICOLOR.

Columba bicolor, Scop. Del. Fl. et Fauna Insubr. p. 94; Sonn. Voy.
N. G. t. 103.
Carpophaga bicolor, G. R. Gray, Gen. of B. ii. p. 468.
Hab. New Guinea (*Sonnerat*).

CARPOPHAGA SPILORRHOA.

Carpophaga spilorrhoa, G. R. Gray, Proc. Z. S. 1858, p. 186.
Carpophaga luctuosa, Gould, B. of Austr. v. pl. 60.
Columba alba, Müll. ?

This species is distinguished by the feathers of the thighs and
under tail-coverts being spotted near the margins, and the outer
tail-feather with the greater part of the outer web and tip black ;
while in *C. luctuosa* the feathers of the thighs and under tail-coverts
end in deep black, and the outer tail-feather is white throughout,
except on the outer web nearest the base.
a. New Guinea.   Presented by Capt. Sir E. Belcher, C.B., R.N.
b. Aru Islands.   Procured from Mr. Wallace.

CARPOPHAGA PUELLA.

Columba puella, Less. Bull. Univ. des Sc. Nat. 1827, p. 400;
Knip & Prev. Pig. t. 1.
Carpophaga puella, G. R. Gray, List of Gall. B. M. p. 5.
Columba amarantha, Selby.
a. New Guinea (River Oetanata). From the Leyden Museum.

CARPOPHAGA LECHLAUCHERI.

Trerolæma Leclaucheri, Pr. B. Compt. Rend. p. 247.
Carpophaga Leclaucheri, G. R. Gray, List of Col. p. 21.
Ptilonopus Lechlaucheri, Sclater, Proc. L. S. 1858, p. 167.
a. New Guinea. Procured from M. Verreaux.

CARPOPHAGA PINON.

Columba pinon, Quoy et Gaim. Voy. Uranie, t. 28.
Carpophaga pinon, Selby, Nat. Libr. v. p. 119.
Zonœnas pinon, Bp. Consp. Av. p. 37.
Hab. Island of Rawak (*Quoy & Gaimard*).
a, b. Aru Islands. Procured from Mr. Wallace.
c. New Guinea. From Baron Laugier's Collection.
d. New Guinea. Presented by Capt. Blackwood, R.N.

CARPOPHAGA MULLERI.

Columba Mulleri, Temm. Pl. Col. 566.
Carpophaga Mulleri, G. R. Gray, Gen. of B. ii. p. 468.
Zonœnas Mulleri, Reich.
Hab. New Guinea; River Oetanata (*Müller*).
a, b. Aru Islands. Procured from Mr. Wallace.

CARPOPHAGA ZOEÆ.

Columba zoeæ, Less. Voy. Coqu. t. 39.
Carpophaga zoeæ, G. R. Gray, Gen. of B. ii. p. 469.
Zonœnas zoeæ, Reich.
Hab. New Guinea; Havre-Dorey (*Lesson*).
a, b. Aru Islands. Procured from Mr. Wallace.

CARPOPHAGA RUFIGASTRA.

Columba rufigastra, Quoy et Gaim. Voy. Astrol. t. 27.
Hab. New Guinea; Havre-Dorey (*Quoy & Gaimard*).

MACROPYGIA PHASIANELLA.

Columba phasianella, Temm. Pl. Col. 100.
Macropygia phasianella, Gould, B. of Austr. v. pl. 75.
a. Aru Islands. Procured from Mr. Wallace.
Hab. Ké Islands (*Wallace*).

MACROPYGIA DOREYA.

Macropygia Doreya, Pr. B. Consp. Av. ii. p. 57.
Hab. New Guinea.

GEOPELIA HUMERALIS.

Columba humeralis, Temm. Pl. Col. 191.
Geopelia humeralis, Gould, B. of Austr. pl. 72.
Erythrauchæna humeralis, Pr. B. Consp. Av. ii. p. 93.
Hab. New Guinea; Lobo (*Müller*).

CHALCOPHAPS STEPHANI.

Peristera Stephani, Hombr. & Jacq. Voy. au Pôle Sud, t. 38. f. 2.
Chalcophaps Stephani, Reichenb.
Hab. New Guinea, west coast (*Homb. & Jacq.*); Lobo (*Müller*).

TRUGON TERRESTRIS.

Trugon terrestris, Homb. & Jacq. Voy. au Pôle Sud, t. 28. f. 2.
Eutrygon terrestris, Sclater, Proc. L. S. 1858, p. 168.
Hab. New Guinea, west coast (*Homb. & Jacq.*).

CALÆNAS NICOBARICA.

Columba nicobarica, Linn. S. N. i. p. 283.
Calænas nicobarica, G. R. Gray, List of Gen. of B. 1840, p. 59.
a, b. Louisiade Archipelago. Presented by Mr. Macgillivray.

CALÆNAS RUFIGULA.

Peristera rufigula, Homb. & Jacq. Voy. au Pôle Sud, t. 27. f. 1.
Calænas rufigula, G. R. Gray.
Phlegaenas rufigula, Pr. B.
Hab. New Guinea (*Homb. & Jacq.*).

GOURA CORONATA.

Columba coronata, Linn. S. N. i. p. 282.
Goura coronata, Steph. Gen. Zool. xi. 1. p. 120.
a. New Guinea. From the Zoological Society's Collection. Lobo (*Müller*).

GOURA VICTORIÆ.

Goura Victoriæ, Fras. Proc. Z. S. 1844, p. 27.
Goura Steursii, Temm.; G. R. Gray, Gen. of B. ii. p. 479. pl. .
a. New Guinea. From the Zoological Society's Collection.

MEGAPODIDÆ.

TALEGALLUS CUVIERI.

Talegallus Cuvieri, Less. Voy. Coqu. t. 38.
Hab. New Guinea; Havre-Dorey (*Lesson*); Aru Islands (*Wallace*).

MEGAPODIUS REINWARDTII.

Megapodius Reinwardtii, Wagl. Syst. Av. (Additamenta, p. 4).
Megapodius Duperreyii, Less. Voy. Coqu. t. 36.
Hab. New Guinea ; Havre-Dorey (*Lesson*).
a–c. Aru Islands. Procured from Mr. Wallace.
d. Ké Island. Procured from Mr. Wallace.

MEGAPODIUS FREYCINETI.

Megapodius Freycineti, Quoy & Gaim. Voy. Uranie, t. 32.
Hab. Island of Waigiou (*Quoy & Gaimard*).

MEGAPODIUS RUBRIPES.

Megapodius rubripes, Temm. Pl. Col. 411.
a. New Guinea ; River Oetanata (*Müller*).

TETRAONIDÆ.

? COTURNIX NOVÆ GUINEÆ.

Tetrao novæ guineæ, Gm. S. N. i. p. 746.
Oriolus cothurnix, Scop. Del. Fl. et Fauna Insubr. p. 87 ; Sonn.
Voy. N. G. t. 105.
Coturnix novæ guineæ, G. R. Gray, Gen. of B. iii. p. 507.
Hab. New Guinea ? (*Sonnerat*).

STRUTHIONIDÆ.

CASUARIUS EMU ?

Struthio casuarius, Linn. S. N. i. p. 265.
Casuarius emu, Lath.
Casuarius galeatus, Vieill.
Hab. New Guinea ; Havre-Dorey (*Lesson*) ; south-west coast
(*Müller*).
a. Aru Islands. Sternum procured from Mr. Wallace.

CHARADRIADÆ.

ESACUS MAGNIROSTRIS.

Charadrius magnirostris, Lath. Ind. Orn. Suppl. p. lxvi.
Œdicnemus magnirostris, Temm. Pl. Col. 387.
Esacus magnirostris, G. R. Gray, List of Gen. of B. 1841, p. 83.
Hab. New Guinea ; River Oetanata (*Müller*).
a. Aru Islands. Procured from Mr. Wallace.

GLAREOLA ISABELLA.

Glareola Isabella, Vieill.
Glareola grallaria, Temm. ; Gould, B. of Austr. vi. pl. 22.
Hab. New Guinea ; River Oetanata (*Müller*).

CHARADRIUS XANTHOCHEILUS.

Charadrius xanthocheilus, Wagl. Syst. Av. Char. sp. 36 ; Gould, B. of Austr. vi. pl. 13.

Hab. Aru Islands (*Wallace*).

CHARADRIUS INORNATUS.

Hiaticula inornata, Gould, B. of Austr. iv. pl. 19.
Charadrius inornatus, G. R. Gray.

Hab. Oomago Island, Torres Straits (*Ince*) ; New Guinea, west coast (*Gould*) ; Aru Islands (*Wallace*).

STREPSILAS INTERPRES.

Tringa interpres, Linn. S. N. i. p. 248.
Strepsilas interpres, G. R. Gray.

Hab. Rainne's Islets, Torres Straits (*Gould*).

HÆMATOPUS LONGIROSTRIS.

Hæmatopus ostralegus, Müll. Verh. Ethn. p. 21 ?
Hæmatopus longirostris, Vieill. N. Dict. d'Hist. Nat. xv. p. 410.

Hab. Aru Islands (*Wallace*) ; New Guinea (*Müller*).

ARDEIDÆ.

ARDEA NOVÆ GUINEÆ.

Ardea novæ guineæ, Gm. S. N. i. p. 644.
Herodias novæ guineæ, Pr. B. Consp. ii. p. 121.

Hab. New Guinea (*Auct.*).

ARDEA ARUENSIS.

Ardea aruensis, G. R. Gray, Proc. Z. S. 1858, p. 188.

Differs from *Herodias picata,* Gould, by having the feathers of the top of the head and the under surface of the body pure white.

Hab. Aru Islands. Procured from Mr. Wallace.

BOTAURUS HELIOSYLUS.

Ardea heliosylus, Less. Voy. de la Coqu. t. 44.
Ardea (Tigrisoma) heliosylus, Less. Tr. d'Orn. p. 572.
Botaurus heliosylus, Pr. B. Consp. Av. ii. p. 136.

Hab. New Guinea ; Havre-Dorey (*Lesson*).

SCOLOPACIDÆ.

NUMENIUS UROPYGIALIS.

Numenius phæopus, Müll. Verh. Ethn. p. 22 ?
Numenius uropygialis, Gould, B. of Austr. vi. pl. 43.
Numenius minor, Müll.

Hab. New Guinea (*Müller*) ; Aru Islands (*Wallace*).

TOTANUS EMPUSA.

Actitis empusa, Gould, B. of Austr. vi. pl. 35.
Totanus hypoleucus, Müll. Verh. Ethn. p. 22.
Hab. New Guinea (*Müller*).

HIMANTOPUS LEUCOCEPHALUS.

Himantopus leucocephalus, Gould, Proc. Z. S. 1839, p. 44; B. of
Austr. vi. pl. 7.
Hab. New Guinea (*Müller*).

TRINGA ALBESCENS.

Schœniclus albescens, Gould, B. of Austr. ii. pl.   .
Tringa pusilla, Müll. Verh. Ethn. p. 23.
Hab. New Guinea; River Oetanata (*Müller*).

PHALAROPUS HYPERBOREUS.

Tringa hyperborea, Linn. S. N. i. p. 249.
Phalaropus hyperboreus, Cuv.
a. Aru Islands.   Procured from Mr. Wallace.

PALAMEDEIDÆ.

PARRA GALLINACEA.

Parra gallinacea, Temm. Pl. Col. 427.
Hab. New Guinea (*Temminck*).

RALLIDÆ.

EULABEORNIS CASTANEOVENTRIS.

Eulabeornis castaneoventris, Gould, B. of Austr. vi. pl. 78.
a, b. Aru Islands.   Procured from Mr. Wallace.

RALLINA TRICOLOR.

Rallina tricolor, G. R. Gray, Proc. Z. S. 1858, p. 188.

Head, neck, nape and breast rusty red, paler on the throat; back,
wing and abdomen slaty black tinged in some places with olive-brown;
the sides, thighs and under tail-coverts banded with pale rufous;
wings beneath slaty black banded with white; bend of the wings,
both above and below, spotted with rufous white.
Length 10″ 6‴; wings 5″ 6‴.
Hab. Aru Islands (*Wallace*).

LARIDÆ.

STERNA TORRESII.

Sterna Torresii, Gould, B. of Austr. pl.   .
Sterna velox, Rüpp. ?; Müll. Verh. Ethn. p. 125.
Hab. New Guinea, west coast (*Müller*).
a. Aru Islands.   Procured from Mr. Wallace.

STERNA MELANAUCHEN.

Sterna melanauchen, Temm. Pl. Col. 427.
Hab. New Guinea (*Müller*).

PELECANIDÆ.

SULA FIBER.

Pelecanus fiber, Linn. S. N. i. p. 218.
Sula fiber, G. R. Gray, List of B. in B.M. iii. p. 183.
Sula fusca, Gould, B. of Austr. vii. pl. 78.
Hab. Near Ké Island (*Wallace*).

GRACULUS HYPOLEUCUS.

Phalacrocorax leucogaster, Gould, B. of Austr. pl.   .
Graculus leucogaster, G. R. Gray.
Carbo hypoleucus, Brandt.
a. Louisiade Archipelago.   Presented by J. Macgillivray, Esq.

List of Species of NEW GUINEA BIRDS and those of the neighbouring localities.

** denotes those contained in the British Museum from this particular locality.

	New Guinea.	Aru Islands.	Ké Islands.	Louisiade Archipelago.	Waigiou.	Timor laut.	N. Australia to 14° lat. S., P. Essington, C. York, &c.	Islands in Torres Strait.
Cuncuma leucogaster	...	*	...	...	...	...	**	*
Haliastur leucosternus	...	*	...	**	...	...	**	*
sphenurus	...	...	...	...	...	...	**	
Pandion leucocephalus	...	...	...	...	...	...	**	*
Jeracidea berigora	...	...	...	...	...	...	*	
Falco frontatus	...	...	...	...	...	...	...	*
Milvus affinis	...	...	...	...	...	...	*	
Baza stenozona	...	*						
Astur novæ hollandiæ	*	...	...	...	...	...	...	**
longicauda	*							
radiatus	...	...	...	...	...	...	**	
approximans	...	...	...	...	...	...	*	
Accipiter poliocephalus	...	*						
cirrhocephalus	...	...	...	...	...	...	*	*
Circus assimilis	...	...	...	...	...	...	...	**
Athene humeralis	*							
theomacha	*							
boobook	...	...	...	...	...	...	**	
rufa	...	...	...	...	...	...	*	
maculata	...	...	...	...	...	...	*	
Strix delicatula	...	...	...	...	...	...	*	*
personata	...	...	...	...	...	...	**	
Podargus papuensis	*	...	...	...	...	...	**	
ocellatus	*	*	...	...	...	...		
marmoratus	...	...	...	...	...	...	**	
phalænoides	...	...	...	...	...	...	**	
Ægotheles leucogaster	...	...	...	...	...	...	**	
Caprimulgus macrurus	...	**	...	...	...	...	*	
Eurostopodus albigularis	...	...	...	...	...	...	*	**
guttatus	...	...	...	...	...	...	**	**
Cypselus australis	...	...	...	...	...	...	**	*
Macropteryx mystaceus	**	**						
Acanthylis caudacuta	...	...	...	...	...	...	**	*
Collocalia hypoleuca	...	*						
nidifica, var.	...	...	...	**				
Hirundo frontalis	*	...	...	...	...	...	...	*
nigricans	...	**						
Eurystomus gularis	**							
pacificus	...	**						
Coracias papuensis	*							
Peltops Blainvilleii	*							
Dacelo Leachii	...	...	...	...	...	...	*	
cervinus	...	...	...	...	...	...	**	
undulatus, Sonn. 106	*							
?, Sonn. 107	*							
Tyro	...	**						
Gaudichaudi	**	**	...	...	*			
macrorhynchus	*							

TABLE (continued).

	New Guinea.	Aru Islands.	Ké Islands.	Louisiade Archipelago.	Waigiou.	Timor laut.	N. Australia to 14° lat. S., P. Essington, C. York, &c.	Islands in Torres Strait.
Halcyon collaris........................	...	*						
albicilla	**	...	...	**				
sancta	...	**	...	...	...	...	**	*
cinnamomina.....................	*							
sordida	...	**	...	...	...	...	*	*
MacLeayi	...	...	...	...	...	...	**	*
Syma flavirostris	...	...	...	...	...	...	**	
torotoro.........................	*	*						
Tanysiptera Dea	**							
Hydrocharis	...?	**						
sylvia	*?	...	...	...	...	...	**	
Ceyx lepida	*							
solitaria	*	*						
(meningting, *Less.*)								
pusilla	*	**	...	...	...	...	**	
Alcyone azurea, var.	*	**	...	...	...	...	**	
Merops ornatus	...	...	...	...	...	...	**	*
Epimachus maximus	**							
albus	**							
magnificus.....................	**	...	...	...	...	...	**	
Nectarinia aspasia	*	*						
zenobia	*	...	*					
frenata	*	**	...	...	...	...	...	*
? australis	...	...	...	...	...	•••	**	
amasia	*							
eximia	*							
eques	*	...	*	...	*			
Arachnothera novæ guineæ	**	**						
Dicæum papuense..................	*							
pectorale	*							
hirundinaceum	...	...	...	...	...	...	**	*
ignicolle	...	**						
Prionichilus niger	*	**						
Myzomela nigrita	...	**						
chermesina	**?							
erythrocephala	...	**	...	...	...	...	*	*
obscura	...	...	...	...	...	...	**	*
pectoralis	...	...	...	...	...	...	*	
sanguinolenta	...	...	...	...	...	...	*	
Glyciphila fasciata..................	...	...	...	...	...	...	**	
modesta.......................	...	*						
ocularis	*	**	...	...	...	...	**	
Ptilotis flaviventris	*							
(chrysotis, *Less.*)								
filigera	...	**	...	...	...	...	**	
unicolor.......................	...	...	...	...	...	...	**	
similis	*	**						
megarhynchus	...	*						
fumata	*							
? striolata	*							

TABLE (continued).

	New Guinea.	Aru Islands.	Ké Islands.	Louisiade Archipelago.	Waigiou.	Timor laut.	N. Australia to 14° lat. S., P. Essington, C. York, &c.	Islands in Torres Strait.
? Ptilotis auriculata	*							
chrysotis	...	...	...	...	...	...	*	*
flavescens	...	...	...	...	...	...	**	
flava	...	...	...	...	...	...	*	
Tropidorhynchus mitratus	*							
nov. guineæ	*	**						
plumigenis	...	...	*					
argenteiceps	...	...	...	...	...	...	**	
citreogularis, var.	...	...	...	...	...	...	*	
chrysotis	*							
vulturinus	...	...	...	...	...	...	*	
buceroides	...	...	...	...	...	...	**	
Eutomophila albigularis	*	...	...	...	...	...	**	
rufogularis	...	...	...	...	...	...	*	
Entomyza albipennis	...	...	...	...	...	...	**	
Melithreptus albogularis	...	...	...	...	...	...	**	
Climacteris melanotus	...	...	...	...	...	...	**	
Sittella leucoptera	...	...	...	...	...	...	**	
Cisticola lineocapilla	...	...	...	...	...	...	**	*
ruficeps	...	...	...	...	...	...	**	**
Sphenœacus galactotes	...	...	...	...	...	...	*	*
Cincloramphus cantillans	...	...	...	...	...	...	*	
Malurus amabilis	...	...	...	...	...	...	*	
Browni	...	...	...	...	...	...	**	
Gerygone chrysogaster	...	**						
magnirostris	...	...	...	...	...	...	*	
lævigaster	...	...	...	...	...	...	*	
chloronotus	...	...	...	...	...	...	*	
Zosterops citrinella	...	...	**	...	...	...	...	*
(albiventris, H. & J.)								
griseotincta	...	...	...	**				
lutea	...	...	...	...	..	...	**	*
Petroica bicolor ?	...	...	...	...	...	...	**	*
Drymodes superciliaris	...	...	...	...	...	...	**	
Grallina australis	...	...	...	...	...	...	*	
Anthus australis	...	...	...	...	...	...	*	
Eupetes Ajax	*							
cærulescens	*							
Brachypteryx murinus	*							
Alcippe monacha	...	**						
Pitta Mackloti	*	**						
novæ guineæ	*	**						
strepitans	...	...	...	...	...	...	*	*
iris	...	...	...	...	...	...	**	
Oriolus Mulleri	*	**						
striatus	**							
assimilis	...	...	...	...	...	...	*	
viridis	...	...	...	...	...	...	**	
flavocinctus	...	...	...	...	...	...	**	
affinis	...	...	...	...	...	...	*	

Table (continued).

	New Guinea.	Aru Islands.	Ké Islands.	Louisiade Archipelago.	Waigiou.	Timor laut.	N. Australia to 14° lat. S., P. Essington, C. York, &c.	Islands in Torres Strait.
Oriolus aureus	**							
?? anais	*							
Sphecotheres flaviventris	...	...	...	...	...	...	**	
Pomatorhinus Isidori	**							
rubecula	...	...	...	...	...	...	**	
Machærirhynchus flaviventris	...	...	...	...	...	...	**	
xanthogenys			**					
Myiagra latirostris	...	**	...	...	...	...	*	
concinna	...	...	...	...	...	...	**	*
(grisea, *H. & J.*)								
lucida	...	...	...	**				
Piezorhynchus nitidus	...	...	...	...	...	...	**	*
rufolateralis	...	**						
Todopsis cyanocephala	*	**						
Tchitrea Gaimardi	*							
Rhipidura threnothorax	*							
rufiventris	*							
hyperythra	...	*						
gularis	*							
isura	...	...	...	...	...	...	**	
assimilis	...	...	**					
maculipectus	...	**						
motacilloides	...	...	...	...	...	...	**	
atripennis	...	**						
rufifrons	...	...	...	...	...	...	**	*
Seisura inquieta	...	...	...	...	...	...	*	
Monarcha carinata	...	...	...	...	...	...		
inornata	*	**						
guttula	*	**						
griseogularis	...	**						
leucura	...	...	**					
trivirgata	...	...	...	...	...	...	**	*
melanoptera	...	...	...	**				
leucotis	...	...	...	**	...	...		
telescophthalma	**	**						
chrysomela	*	**						
Kaupi	...	...	...	...	...	...	*	
Micrœca flavovirescens	...	**						
flavigaster	...	...	...	...	...	...	*	
Pardalotus luctuosus	...	...	...	...	...	...	*	
melanocephalus	...	...	...	...	...	...	**	
Smicrornis flavescens	...	...	...	...	...	...	*	
Pachycephala griseiceps	...	**						
rufipennis	...	...	**					
monacha	...	**						
? lugubris	*							
? virescens	*							
melanura	...	...	...	...	...	...	**	**
spinicauda	*						**	*
falcata	...	...	...	...	...	...	**	*

TABLE (continued).

	New Guinea.	Aru Islands.	Ké Islands.	Louisiade Archipelago.	Waigiou.	Timor laut.	N. Australia to 14° lat. S., P. Essington, C. York, &c.	Islands in Torres Strait.
Pachycephala simplex	...	...	***	...	...	...	**	
Hylocharis ——, *Müll.*	*					...		
Campephaga Desgrazii	*							
Boyeri	*							
cæruleogrisea	...	*						
melanops	...	**	...	...	...	...	*	*
hypoleuca	...	*	...	**	...	...	*	
melas	*							
plumbea	*							
novæ guineæ	*							
papuensis	*							
schisticeps	*							
Swainsoni	...	...	...	...	...	...	*	
Jardinii	...	...	...	...	...	...	*	
rufiventris	*?	...	...	...	...	...	**	*
(Karu, *Gould.*)								
polygrammica	...	**						
Artamus papuensis	*	*						
minor	...	...	...	...	...	...	**	
leucopygialis	...	...	...	...	...	...	**	*
albiventris	...	...	...	...	...	...	*	
Dicrurus bracteatus	...	...	...	...	...	...	**	*
assimilis	...	**						
megalornis	...	...	*					
megarhynchus	*							
carbonarius	*							
Rectes kirrocephalus	**							
dichrous	*	**						
strepitans	*	**						
Colluriocincla brunnea	...	...	...	...	...	...	**	*
harmonica	...	...	...	...	...	...	*	
parvula	...	...	...	...	...	...	**	
Myiolestes megarhynchus	**							
aruensis	...	**						
griseatus	...	...	...	...	...	...	**	
pulverulentus	*							
Cracticus cassicus	*							
personatus	...	**						
nigrogularis	...	...	...	...	...	...	*	
Quoyi	*	**	...	...	...	...	**	
picatus	...	...	...	...	...	...	**	
argentatus	...	...	...	...	...	...	*	
Corvus orru	*	**						
(macrorhynchus, pt., *Wagl.*)								
corone, pt., *Wagl.*	*							
coronoides	...	...	...	...	...	...	*	*
Gymnocorvus senex	*							
Paradisea apoda	**							
var. Wallaciana	...	**						
papuensis	**							

TABLE (continued).

	New Guinea.	Aru Islands.	Ké Islands.	Louisiade Archipelago.	Waigiou.	Timor laut.	N. Australia to 14° lat. S., P. Essington, C. York, &c.	Islands in Torres Strait.
Paradisea regia	**	**						
speciosa	**							
atra	**							
sexpennis	**							
rubra	...	...	...	...	*			
?? Wilsoni	*							
Astrapia nigra	**							
carunculata	*							
Ptilonorhynchus buccoides	*							
melanotis		**						
Chlamydera cerviniventris	...	...	...	...	...	...	**	*
Manucodia viridis	**	**						
atra	*							
Keraudrenii	*	...	...	...	...	...	**	
Lamprotornis viridescens	...	**						
metallica	...	...	...	...	...	...	**	
Gracula Dumontii	**	**						
Donacola castaneothorax	...	...	...	...	...	...	*	*
flaviprymna	...						**	
Estrelda annulosa	...	...	...	...	...	...	**	
Phaëton	...	...					**	
Amadina castanotis	...	...	...	...	...	...	**	
Gouldiæ	...	...	...	...	...	...	**	
mirabilis	...	...	...	...	...	...	**	
Poephila acuticauda	...	...	...	...	...	...	**	
personata	...	...	...	...	...	...	**	
Buceros ruficollis	*	...	...	...	*			
Platycercus dorsalis	**							
palliceps	...	...	...	...	...	...	**	
cyanogenys	...	...	...	...	...	...	**	
Brownii	...	...	...	...	...	...	*	
Aprosmictus erythropterus, var.	*	...	...	...	...	...	**	
Charmosyna papua	**							
Lorius domicella	*							
tricolor	*	...	...	**				
puniceus	*							
Eos squamata	*							
atra	*							
scintillata	*							
rubrifrons	...	**						
rubiginosa	...	...	...	...	**			
Eclectus Linnæi	...	**						
polychloros	*	...	...	...	*			
var. aruensis	...	**						
paraguanus	...	...	...	...	*			
Tarabe	*							
Coriphilus placentis	**	*						
Trichoglossus Swainsonii	...	...	...	...	...	...	...	*
rubritorquis	...	...	...	...	...	...	*	
cyanogrammus	*							

TABLE (continued).

	New Guinea.	Aru Islands.	Ké Islands.	Louisiade Archipelago.	Waigiou.	Timor laut.	N. Australia to 14° lat. S., P. Essington, C. York, &c.	Islands in Torres Strait.
Trichoglossus coccineifrons	...	*						
nigrogularis	...	**						
versicolor	...	...	...	...	...	...	**	
? Tanygnathus marginatus	*							
? macrorhynchus	*							
Psittacus personatus	*							
Pucherani	*							
capistratus	...	...	**					
aruensis	...	**						
Psittacula diophthalmus	*	**						
Desmarestii	*							
Nasiterna pygmæa	*							
Cacatua æquatorialis	*							
(C. sulphurea?)								
Triton	*	*						
(C. galerita.)								
? galerita	...	...	...	...	...	...	*	*
sanguinea	...	...	...	...	...	...	*	
Calyptorhynchus macrorhynchus	...	...	...	...	...	...	*	
Microglossum aterrimum	**	**	...	...	*	...	**	
Alecto	*							
Dasyptilus Pecquetii	*							
? Chrysocolaptes cardinalis	*							
Centropus Menebiki	*	**						
spilopterus	...	*						
phasianus (macrourus)	...	...	...	...	...	...	**	*
Eudynamys punctatus	*							
(rufiventris, *Less.*)								
Flindersii	...	...	...	...	...	...	**	*
Cuculus leucolophus	*							
assimilis	...	*						
megarhynchus	...	*						
dumetorum	...	...	...	...	...	...	*	
Chrysococcyx lucidus	*	...	...	...	...	...	*	
Ptilonopus superbus	...	**	...	...	...	...	*	*
Rivoli	*							
strophium	...	...	...	**				
prasinorrhous	...	...	**					
perlatus	*	**						
Wallacii	...	**						
pulchellus	**							
cyanovirens	**							
virens	*							
aurantiifrons	...	**						
coronulatus	...	**						
nainus	*							
iozonus	...	**						
viridis	*							
Ewingii	...	...	...	...	...	...	**	
Carpophaga Pinon	**	**	...	...	*			

TABLE (continued).

	New Guinea.	Aru Islands.	Ké Islands.	Louisiade Archipelago.	Waigiou.	Timor laut.	N. Australia to 14° lat. S., P. Essington, C. York, &c.	Islands in Torres Strait.
Carpophaga Zoeæ	*	**						
Mulleri	*	**						
? bicolor	*							
spilorrhoa	**	**	...	...	...	...	**	
chalybura	...	**						
Sundevalii	...	...	...	**				
pacifica	*							
(ænea, *Auct.*)								
? myristicivora	*							
albogularis	*	...	...	**				
rufigaster	*							
puella	**							
assimilis	...	...	...	...	...	...	**	
Leclaucheri	**							
Lopholaimus antarcticus	...	...	...	...	...	...	*	
Macropygia phasianella	...	**						
Doreya	*							
Reinwardtii	*							
Geopelia humeralis	*	...	...	...	...	...	**	*
tranquilla (?)	...	...	...	...	...	...	*	*
placida	...	...	...	...	...	...	**	
Chalcophaps chrysochlora	...	...	...	...	...	...	**	
Stephani	*							
Petrophassa albipennis	...	...	...	...	...	...	**	
Peristera chalcoptera	...	...	...	...	...	...	**	
histrionica	...	...	...	...	...	...	*	
Trugon terrestris	*							
Geophaps Smithii	...	...	...	...	...	...	**	
Lophophaps plumifera	...	...	...	...	...	...	**	
Calænas nicobarica	...	...	...	**				
rufigula	*							
Goura coronata	**							
Victoriæ	**							
Talegallus Cuvieri	*							
Lathami	...	...	...	...	...	...	**	
Megacephalon maleo	*							
Megapodius Duperreyii	*	**						
Freycineti	*	...	...	...	*			
rubripes	*							
tumulus	...	...	...	...	...	...	**	*
? Coturnix novæ guineæ	*							
pectoralis	...	...	...	...	...	...	*	
australis	...	...	...	...	...	...	*	*
sinensis	...	...	...	...	...	...	...	*
Turnix melanota	...	...	...	...	...	...	*	*
castanota	...	...	...	...	...	...	**	
Casuarius emu	*	*						
australis	...	...	...	...	...	...	*	
Dromaius novæ hollandiæ	...	...	...	...	...	...	*	
Esacus magnirostris	*	**	...	...	...	...	*	*

TABLE (continued).

	New Guinea.	Aru Islands.	Ké Islands.	Louisiade Archipelago.	Waigiou.	Timor laut.	N. Australia to 14° lat., S., P. Essington, C. York, &c.	Islands in Torres Strait.
Glareola grallaria	*							
Lobivanellus personatus	...	...	...	...	...	...	**	
Charadrius xanthocheilus	...	*	...	...	...	...	**	*
veredus	...	...	...	...	...	...	*	
ruficapillus	...	...	...	...	...	...	*	*
inornatus	*?	*	...	...	...	...	*	*
Cinclus interpres	*	...	...	...	...	...	*	*
Hæmatopus longirostris	...	*	...	...	...	...	**	*
fuliginosus	...	...	...	...	...	...	*	*
Grus australasianus	...	...	...	...	...	...	*	
Ardea rectirostris	...	...	...	...	...	...	**	
pacifica	...	...	...	...	...	...	*	
nov. guineæ	*							
jugularis	*?	...	...	...	...	...	**	*
? Greyii	...	...	...	**	...	...	**	*
plumifera	...	...	...	...	...	...	*	*
syrmatophora	...	...	...	...	...	...	...	*
immaculata	...	...	...	...	...	...	*	
picata	...	...	...	...	...	...	**	
aruensis	...	*						
Nycticorax caledonicus	...	...	...	...	...	...	**	*
Ardetta stagnatilis	*	...	...	...	...	...	*	*
(virescens, *Auct.*)								
flavicollis	...	...	...	...	...	...	*	
Botaurus heliosyla	*							
Mycteria australis	...	...	...	...	...	...	*	
Threskiornis strictipennis	...	...	...	...	...	...	*	
Falcinellus igneus	...	...	...	...	...	...	**	
Platalea regia	...	...	...	...	...	...	**	
Numenius uropygialis	...	*	...	...	...	...	**	*
(phæopus ?)								
australis	...	...	...	...	...	...	**	*
minutus	...	...	...	...	...	...	*	
Limosa uropygialis	...	...	...	...	...	...	**	*
melanuroides	...	...	...	...	...	...	*	
Xenus cinereus	...	...	...	...	...	...	**	
Totanus glottoides	...	...	...	...	...	...	**	*
griseopygius	...	...	...	...	...	...	**	
Tringoides empusa	*	...	...	...	...	...	*	
(hypoleucus ?)								
Himantopus leucocephalus	*	...	...	...	...	...	**	
(candidus ?)								
Tringa albescens	*	...	...	...	...	...	*	*
(pusilla ?)								
australis	...	...	...	...	...	...	**	*
Scolopax australis	...	...	...	...	...	...	*	
Phalaropus hyperboreus, var.	...	**						
Parra gallinacea	*	...	...	...	...	...	**	
Rallina tricolor	...	*						
Rallus pectoralis	...	...	...	...	...	...	**	*

TABLE (continued).

	New Guinea.	Aru Islands.	Ké Islands.	Louisiade Archipelago.	Waigiou.	Timor laut.	N. Australia to 14° lat., S., P. Essington, C. York, &c.	Islands in Torres Strait.
Porzana leucophrys	...	...	...	...	...	...	...	*
Eulabeornis castaneoventris	...	**	...	...	...	...	*	
Porphyrio melanotus	...	...	...	...	...	...	**	*
Anseranus melanoleucus	...	...	...	...	...	...	**	
Nettapus pulchellus	...	...	...	...	...	...	**	
Tadorna radjah	...	...	...	...	...	...	**	
Dendrocygna arcuata	...	...	...	...	...	...	*	
Leptotarsis Eytoni	...	...	...	...	...	...	**	
Anas punctata	...	...	...	...	...	...	**	
Nyroca australis	...	...	...	...	...	...	*	
Podiceps gularis	...	...	...	...	...	...	**	
? Eudyptes torquata	*							
? papua	*							
? Aptenodytes longirostris (?)	*							
Puffinus sphenurus	...	...	...	...	...	...	...	*
Xema Jamesonii ?	...	...	...	...	...	...	*	*
Sterna strenuus	...	...	...	...	...	...	*	
pelecanoides	...	...	...	...	...	...	**	*
Torresii (velox, *Auct.* ?)	...	**	...	...	...	...	*	*
gracilis	...	...	...	...	...	...	*	
melanauchen	*	...	...	...	...	...	**	*
nereis	...	...	...	...	...	...	*	*
fuliginosa	...	...	...	...	...	...	*	*
panaya	...	...	...	...	...	...	**	*
Gygis candida	...	...	...	...	...	...	*	
Hydrochelidon fluviatilis	...	...	...	...	...	...	*	
Anoüs stolidus	...	...	...	...	...	...	*	*
leucocapillus	...	...	...	...	...	...	*	*
Phaëton phœnicurus	...	...	...	...	...	...	...	*
Sula fiber	...	*	...	...	...	...	*	**
piscator	...	...	...	...	...	...	*	**
personata	...	...	...	...	...	...	...	*
Pelecanus conspicillatus	...	...	...	...	...	...	**	*
Graculus hypoleucus	...	...	...	**				
melanoleucus	...	...	...	...	...	...	*	*
Attagen ariel	...	...	...	...	...	...	**	*

ERRATUM.

Page 28, *for* Rhipidura maculi*pennis read* R. maculi*pectus*.